# MEATBALLS, MAFIA, AND MURDER

## AN ITALIAN-AMERICAN COZY MYSTERY SERIES
### BOOK 4

### M.P. BLACK

*For, you, the reader. Thank you.*

**1**

"Frankie Fazio shot Vinnie Albanese three times. Between the silencer on his gun and the neighbor's thumping music, nobody heard. Frankie left the rival mobster on the bed. Vinnie, for once, looked peaceful. On his way out of the apartment, Frankie caught sight of the pot on the stove and stopped. He lifted the lid and raised the wooden spoon to his mouth. He winced. 'Vinnie, you *stunad*, why'd you go and use those cheap tomatoes? You ruined the sauce.'"

Marco Puglisi, bestselling author of the Frankie F. mafia thrillers, closed his latest book.

The audience at Milano Books, which had been so quiet during the reading that you could've heard a pin drop, burst into enthusiastic applause.

Puglisi, a tiny man with giant glasses, smiled. His teeth were large, too, which made his face look donkey-like. If donkeys wore bifocals. His glasses kept slipping, and he pushed them up to the bridge of his nose as he thanked the audience.

On the table in front of Peewee sat a stack of hardbacks.

One copy rested against a book stand, revealing the dark, gritty cover and the bold title: *Sicilians Wear Black.*

I leaned close to Angelica, keeping my voice low.

"His books seem so ..." I looked for the right word. "*Muscular*. I expected a tough guy. But Puglisi's nothing like the mobsters he writes about."

"Everyone calls him 'Peewee,'" she said. "Ever since he was a kid, he's been called that. Even when he taught English at Carmine High. And no amount of fame will change that."

Looking over at Peewee Puglisi, I caught sight of Phil Palladino, who sat next to him. Phil owned Milano Books, the only bookstore in Carmine, New Jersey, and he'd been so nervous in the days before this big Saturday night event that he must've bought every antacid on the shelf at Martini's Italian Market.

Now he gave me a big smile and a thumbs up. That made me happy. I knew how much tonight meant to him. Plus, it was good exposure for all of Carmine's businesses.

Peewee, a Carmine native, had gained national fame with his hard-boiled tales of a mafia hitman, and in addition to attracting many locals, the event had brought journalists and readers from New York City. Milano Books was packed.

There was the kind of buzz tonight you might expect at a Christmas party. I imagined book events in the city were more formal, more muted. But this was an excuse for Carmine to celebrate one of its own, showcasing that even our little town could produce a bestselling author.

Phil adjusted his cardigan and got to his feet. After giving profuse thanks to the author by his side, he said, "Mr. Puglisi will sign your books now, so please line up."

People got up from the rows of chairs facing Peewee's table. Over the din of chairs scraping and people talking,

Phil raised his voice: "Oh, and if you want nibbles and drinks, our speakeasy is open."

He chuckled as he gestured toward Angelica and me.

Our food station, a couple of paces from Peewee's table, had a sign that said, "Moroni's Speakeasy." We both wore black shirts with white ties, white suspenders, and pin-striped pants in a nod to 1920s mafia outfits. It didn't matter that Peewee's books had a more contemporary setting—the guests got a kick out of the costumes.

"I wore a costume just like that last Halloween," Sofia Ruggiero told me.

"Costume?" her friend, Rose Calabrese said, a mischievous glint in her eye. "Those were clothes from your youth."

Sofia swatted her friend, and together, they cackled at the joke. The two ladies, both soon to be celebrating their 80th birthday, never failed to put a smile on my face.

"Angelica," Rose said, studying the food on display. "You've outdone yourself again."

She was right, of course. At a typical book reading, guests would be lucky to get a glass of tepid tap water and a few stale pretzel sticks. But Angelica, owner of Moroni's Italian Bakery, and also my boss and friend, had prepared an enticing spread.

There was a platter with *bruschetta*, made with Angelica's own fresh-baked bread and topped with fresh, chopped tomatoes and basil. She'd made tiny pastry puffs stuffed with ricotta and roasted red peppers, nicely complemented by miniature meatballs on skewers, courtesy of her brother, Carlo, who owned Carmine's best restaurant. A cheese platter with a variety of hard cheeses offered easily held finger food. And guests could choose from several non-alcoholic drinks: a sparkling lemonade with ginger; a pitcher of lemon, mint, and cucumber-infused water; and a red drink

—a raspberry spritzer—which Angelica had dubbed a "Carmine Bloody Mary."

While Angelica and I were busy serving food and drinks to guests, my friend Nat Natale was also busy. As an employee of the public library and Carmine historical society, he'd had the clever idea of setting up a table with "mafia artifacts." He and his boss, Mrs. Viola, explained the history of the objects to anyone interested. Many were. The table stood near the checkout counter, and it had drawn as many people as our "speakeasy" station.

An hour or so later, the line for the book signing grew shorter and the crowd at our food station thinned out. Angelica put together a plate with bruschetta, meatballs, and the ricotta puffs, and handed it to me.

"Bernie, *mia cara*, why don't you take this over to Nat and Mrs. Viola? We don't want them to go hungry."

I smiled.

Angelica was a beautiful person. On the inside and the outside. Chocolate-brown eyes. Black hair with a single white streak, caught up in a complex architecture of hairpins. And a smile that could melt an ice cube's heart.

Her greatest worry in life seemed to be that people wouldn't get their fair share of Italian food.

"Go," she said. "Go."

So I went. And I was halfway across the room, thinking of what the world would look like if we didn't have people like Angelica, when I stopped dead.

Startled, and nearly dropping the plate of appetizers, I stared across the room.

By the bookstore entrance, leaning against the doorframe, was a person I knew well. She wore a baseball cap, pulled down low over her eyes. Yet I had no doubt: It was U.S. Marshall Roberta LaRosa.

It was thanks to Roberta that I'd landed in Carmine, New Jersey. Before my current life as Bernie Smyth, assistant baker and barista at Moroni's Italian Bakery, I had been the famous actress Bernadette Kovac. I starred as Eve Silver in America's favorite detective show on TV, *Silver & Gold*. That had all ended when I testified against my co-star, Jay Casanova, in his drug- and arms-trafficking trial, and had to go into witness protection.

Roberta had placed me in Carmine, and once the threat to my life passed, I'd chosen to stay in this wonderful town, even holding on to the identity Roberta had given me: Goodbye, actress Bernadette Kovac—hello, Bernie Smyth, barista and assistant baker!

But since I'd left witness protection, Roberta and I didn't officially have anything to do with each other anymore. Still, she'd appeared in Carmine before. And that had been a sign of trouble.

I changed direction and headed toward her.

She was staring across the room, intent on someone else. Glancing over my shoulder, I tried to guess who she was so interested in. Was it someone in line to have their book signed? Or someone near the food station?

I turned my attention back to Roberta. But the space by the doorframe was empty.

Roberta had vanished.

Outside the bookstore windows, the streetlights along Garibaldi Avenue, Carmine's main street, glowed softly in the dark evening. Rain sparkled in the light and ran down the glass. And as I gazed out, a USPS truck rumbled past.

For as long as I'd known Roberta, she'd moved around incognito in a USPS truck, making "deliveries" at the most unexpected times.

I sighed. Whatever Roberta was up to, I hoped it wouldn't interfere with tonight's event. There'd been enough crime and murder in Carmine lately, and each time I'd been pulled into the investigation. For once, I wanted to stick to being Angelica's assistant.

I headed for the historical society's table.

Nat's fair hair fell over his round, steel-rimmed glasses. He swept his bangs aside and smiled. He was thrilled to see me—and not just because I'd brought provisions.

"Hey, Bernie, did you see what we put together for our display?"

I wasn't the only person craning forward to take a closer look. The display was a hit. And no wonder—because in addition to black-and-white photos of Carmine's early days, plus snapshots of "Carmine's most famous killers and crooks," the display included several intriguing items from Carmine's less cozy past: a Tommy gun, one of those classic gangster submachine guns with the distinctive drum magazine; a police helmet and billy club; a garrote wire for strangling; a hatchet, which I feared had not been used to chop wood; and a switchblade called the Italian stiletto.

"Don't worry," Nat said, as I handed him the plate with food. "The barrel of the Tommy gun's blocked and the Italian stiletto's a prop from a Broadway show. It couldn't cut butter on a hot summer's day."

The hatchet looked sharp, though. And I reached out to touch the blade.

"No touching," Mrs. Viola snapped, and I pulled back my hand, as if burned.

Mrs. Viola, Head Curator of the Carmine Historical

Appreciation & Preservation Society, looked as stiff as one of Madame Tussaud's wax figures. She stood a few feet behind the table, her arms crossed, and eyed everyone approaching the table with a suspicious glare.

Near her stood two people I didn't know, speaking in low voices. The woman had red hair cut into a severe bob, and her mouth curved downward in a frown. She held a briefcase in one hand. The burly man next to her reminded me of a missionary. If that missionary lifted a lot of weights. Guess it was his buzz cut, formal jacket, and white button-down shirt with a drab tie, everything so neatly pressed and buttoned up that he looked ready for church.

"These objects are great," I said to Nat and Mrs. Viola, while actually thinking what a nightmare this was.

*Roberta LaRosa appears and disappears, and now there's a table-full of murder weapons? Mamma mia.*

The flash from a camera went off next to me, and it made me jump. I turned to see Peter Piatek snapping photos of the display. Peter and I knew each other well. He ran the *Carmine Enquirer*, an online news site, and he had a passion for getting clicks on articles.

"We should get a shot of Marco Puglisi holding the Tommy gun."

"Over my dead body," the red-headed woman said.

Peter smiled. "You must be Anne Adams, Puglisi's agent."

"Agent, promoter, publicist, you name it, I do it all."

"Almost all," the big man next to her said.

She shrugged. "Nino here is Mr. Puglisi's so-called research assistant."

"If you don't like the Tommy gun," Peter said to Anne, "how about the hatchet?"

"A gun with a silencer—that's the only prop that makes sense. Have you even read the Frankie F. books?"

Nino put a hand on her arm and whispered, "Easy, Anne."

But Peter, apparently seeing an opportunity to talk to the author himself, had lost interest and moved on.

"Don't patronize me, Nino." Anne shook off his arm, and looked around at the bookstore with a sour expression on her face. "I can't believe I'm back in Carmine. I vowed never to set foot in this dump again. But the great Marco Puglisi, in spite of his unrivaled writing talent, can't pull himself away from this Podunk town."

"What's eating you, Anne?"

She didn't answer him. Instead, she strode across the room toward Peewee, who was still signing books. Nino set his jaw and trudged after her.

I was torn. I should head straight back to Angelica and help her, but even as I was telling myself that, my feet turned toward Anne and Nino. I took a step in their direction. Then stopped. Took a step toward Angelica, and stopped.

Nat laughed and leaned toward me. "Go ahead, Bernie. You know your curiosity will always win."

I groaned. "You can read me like an open book."

"Hey, I spend a lot of time at the public library—my reading skills are excellent." He winked at me. "Besides, I've seen you do this before. Go ahead. Snoop around a little. It won't kill you."

"Angelica needs me."

"Angelica's fine," he said. "Go."

With Nat's blessing, I allowed myself to take a detour.

*After this, I'll head straight back to Angelica and help with the appetizers and drinks. Promise.*

Peewee signed another book with a flourish and pushed his glasses up his nose.

Next, a man and a woman stepped forward. The woman had dark hair and a tentative smile, and she was the one who clutched one of Peewee's books.

Peewee cocked his head. "Don't I know you?"

She shook her head.

"We're visiting family," the man said, answering the question. "I went to Carmine High and actually took your English class. You can inscribe the book to me, Roberto Rizzoli."

"Roberto Rizzoli? Of course, now I recognize you. You're Anne's—"

"Ex," Anne cut in.

She stepped closer to the table.

Roberto greeted her with a nod.

"Anne," he said.

"Roberto," she said. "Did you come to gloat?"

"We came to make peace."

"We? Oh, you mean you and your little *lady*?" Only she didn't use the word lady. She used a very un-ladylike word for lady. "What, breaking up my marriage wasn't enough? Did you tell your friends about how you met this woman on one of your business trips?"

"You know that's not what happened ..." Roberto sighed. "Let's forget it. We're visiting my mother and I asked Gina to come with me. That's all."

Just then, Phil interrupted with an announcement. The book signing was officially ending and Milano Books would be closing. There was much hubbub as guests said their goodbyes to Peewee and Phil, many thanking Angelica as well, and people streamed out into the street. Phil reminded Peewee that he'd arranged drinks and food for private guests after the bookstore closed. As the last people left the store, Roberto reached out and put a hand on Anne's arm and said, "Anne, we need to go."

"Stick around for the party, Rob. I'd love to get a chance to talk to your lovely wife."

She gave Gina a smile that would've made a cobra proud. Gina recoiled.

"That's generous of you, Anne," Roberto said, either unaware or willfully ignoring what had obviously been more of a threat than an invitation. "I hope we can put our past behind us. As you know, *Blessed are the peacemakers, for they will be called the children of God.*"

Anne laughed. There was no joy in her laugh. "Your stupid piety doesn't fool me, Rob. I know the real you. If you could strangle me, you would."

At that very moment, there was a loud snick-snick, and I turned toward the entrance. Phil had locked the front door.

Supposedly, the after-party was a more intimate affair. But Phil's idea of intimate was expansive. Us "crew members," so to speak, consisted of Peewee, Nino (Clemenza, I learned, was his last name), Anne, Phil, Mrs. Viola, Angelica, Nat, and me. Apart from Roberto and his wife, Gina, the other two dozen guests or so were editors, journalists, even a few fellow thriller writers, all connected to the publishing scene in New York City.

Angelica uncorked bottles of wine. People ate more ricotta puffs and meatballs and bruschetta, and they perched on chairs or leaned against bookshelves as they talked. Speakers mounted near the ceiling played music, Louis Prima wishing his signorina a "*buona sera.*" The noise level increased.

Angelica asked me to get more paper plates and cups from the office.

"Oh, and while you're out there," Phil called after me, "can you grab more wine as well, please?"

At the far end of the bookstore were two doors right next to each other—the restroom to the left and the back-room office to the right.

The door was ajar. As I pushed it open, I heard voices, and stopped. It was Peewee and Nino. I could just make out Nino's back from where I stood. Beyond him, a couch was pushed against a wall and to the left of that stood one of the shelves with book inventory.

"She's laying into that vino like there ain't no tomorrow," Peewee, out of sight, was saying. "And her breath reeked of booze when she showed up."

"Everyone has bad days, boss."

"The other day she was like this, too. And then there's the business of her arranging meetings behind my back."

"That was a mistake. I canceled it."

Behind me, I heard Nat call out, "Phil said you might need my help."

I was sure Nino and Peewee had heard him, so I said, "Great," and pushed the door wide open and walked in.

"Oh, hi," I said casually.

As Nat and I headed for the boxes of wine bottles Phil had left next to the inventory shelves at the back, Nino and Peewee headed for the door. Peewee gave me an apologetic smile and said, with a sigh, "Business stuff."

"I understand."

When Nat and I came out of the office, each with a box of wine and paper plates and cups balanced on top, Nino and Peewee had glasses of wine and were talking to guests.

On the surface, everything seemed fine. But my hands tingled. My nose itched, and I wrinkled it.

It was like smelling mold where I couldn't see it—something wasn't right.

I unboxed the bottles of wine and helped Angelica uncork another three bottles. Half a dozen bottles already stood empty on the table, and it seemed Anne was doing her best to polish another off. She jerked back her head, draining her wine glass. Then refilled it at once.

Gina came to the table, and I poured her a glass of wine.

"It's a beautiful bookshop," she said to me, seeming eager to talk.

"Are you a big reader?" I asked.

"Yes, but not thrillers. Not books like Marco Puglisi's."

"Too violent?"

She nodded and explained that she preferred books that focused on making the world a better place. As she talked, I caught sight of Mrs. Viola across the room, glaring at us.

*Now, why is she looking at us as if we stole her favorite book?*

A lot of her personal favorites were spiritual books, Gina was telling me.

"But I'll read anything that will bring more kindness into this world. There's been enough murder and pain—what the world needs is more love."

Anne snorted. She'd been eavesdropping.

"Talk about rose-tinted glasses."

She stumbled toward Gina, knocking into her with the briefcase and sloshing wine down her dress. Even as Gina dabbed her dress with napkins, Anne leaned close and whispered something.

I couldn't make out what it was, but it sounded a lot like, "He'll cheat again."

Whatever it was, the intention was clearly to upset Gina.

And it worked. Gina, who'd seemed high-strung from the moment I met her, set down her glass, nearly knocking it over, and spun around to flee.

Roberto caught her in his arms. Over Gina's head, he glared at Anne.

"You've got a lot of nerve ..." he muttered through clenched teeth.

Anne stared at him. There was a long, icy silence.

Which was broken when Phil, Peewee, and Nino strolled over to the drinks table.

"So, years ago, you had an idea for a book, Nino. Remember that? You still think of writing it?"

Nino shook his head. "Nah. Too busy with my work for Mr. Puglisi."

"Best researcher in the business," Peewee said, and gave Nino a pat on the back.

Peewee grabbed three glasses of wine, handing one to Phil and one to Nino before claiming the third for himself. Then glanced over at Anne. He quickly looked away, apparently reluctant to engage in a conversation with her. He pushed his glasses up to the bridge of his nose.

Phil asked Peewee about his writing process. "Where do you get your inspiration?"

Peewee talked about research, and how there was no end to the inspiration he could get from news articles. But also how he'd had the opportunity to talk to people who'd worked in the mafia. That made me think of Primo Leone, owner of Carmine's only taxi company. Primo was a former driver for the mob. I wondered if Peewee had ever talked to him.

Peewee put an arm around Nino's shoulder. "If it wasn't for Nino's research, I wouldn't be able to write the books. At least not as fast as I do now. My readers are always chomping at the bit for a new installment in the Frankie F. saga. I swear, if I jotted down a bit of Frankie's dialogue on a napkin, it would sell at auction."

He laughed, a donkey's guffaw.

Anne teetered on her heels and nearly fell. She raised her briefcase, brandishing it. "I've got a big ol' napkin right in here ..."

Nino caught her before she toppled over. "Come on, Anne. I think you need to lie down."

"There's a couch in the office," Phil said, a worried look on his face.

With a hand around Anne's back, Nino led her toward the office in the back. She seemed half-unconscious, but as I watched them walk away, something strange happened.

The moment before Nino pulled her through the door to the office, Anne slipped a hand into one of his jacket pockets—very much as if she were pickpocketing him.

Now, why would she do that?

"**A**bsolutely dead," Phil said, and sank onto a chair by the food station. "Dead on my feet."

He took off one of his brogues and massaged his foot.

There was lots of commotion as people found their coats, finished drinks, and went in and out of the restroom —one thriller author drunkenly wandering into the dark back office before realizing his mistake—but now Milano Books was finally quieting down. The last of the guests had left. Phil had locked the door behind them. The only people remaining were the "crew members," plus the Rizzolis.

Angelica and I were cleaning up the food station, which

had turned into a mess of empty glasses and bottles, discarded paper plates, and half-filled cups with water and other beverages. There were also books, picked off shelves for consideration or conversation, and then discarded next to a wine glass.

One of the books was Giuseppe Di Lampedusa's *The Leopard*. Another was Agatha Christie's *Evil Under the Sun*, which I'd read several times. I stacked them on a third book, one of Peewee's called *The Killer's Cabin*, and returned them to their shelves.

Phil said, "I haven't been so nervous since I went on tour with Tarantella."

Before becoming a bookstore owner, Phil had briefly enjoyed one-hit-wonder fame with a hard rock band, in which the big hair was as memorable as the music. It was difficult to imagine that, decades ago, this bald, cardigan-wearing bookseller had once worn purple tights. But then I bet people who knew about my past wondered at the transformation I'd undergone, from TV detective Eve Silver to small-town Bernie Smyth.

"The event was a success," Peewee said, coming back from the restroom. "Don't you think so, Nino?"

Nino nodded.

"You really think so?" Phil said. "Well, I hope it won't be the last time you come to read at Milano Books."

"I'm sure it isn't," Peewee said, smiling his big-toothed smiled and then covering his mouth as he stifled a yawn.

Across the room, Nat and Mrs. Viola were packing up the historical society's artifacts.

"Where's the hatchet?" Mrs. Viola asked.

"I packed it already."

Nat was putting the Tommy gun in a bag on the table.

"Not like that—you'll scratch it," Mrs. Viola said, and she

grabbed the gun and a different bag and began to pack it herself, wrapping it in bubble wrap. "And it goes in this other bag. I didn't track down all these objects, identify them, catalog them, only to have you lose them ..."

Nat watched her, hands on his hips, and a rueful twist to his mouth. I'd never watched him work with Mrs. Viola, and I was amazed he could tolerate her fussiness. But then he was the most even-keeled person I knew. Even as I watched, Nat gave a shrug and started stacking the historical photographs, checking each off an inventory list.

Angelica brought my attention back to the food station.

"All these glasses have to go out back. As do the empty bottles."

I placed the empty bottles in boxes and the glasses on trays, getting ready to carry them out back.

"I'll help you," Nat said, joining me at the table. He leaned close and whispered, "Mrs. Viola has banished me from her kingdom. She says she can't keep track of things if I keep putting them away, and now she's going back over the entire inventory to make sure we haven't missed anything. She's sure I misplaced something."

"Attention to detail," I said.

"That's one word for it."

I picked up a box of wine bottles. Nat grabbed a tray of glasses.

"Here, let me be helpful," Roberto said, picking up a tray as well.

Silently, Nino joined the expedition, picking up a box of wine bottles, and then another, stacking it on top of the first.

At the office door, Nino held his boxes with one strong arm and pushed open the door. It was pitch black inside, and yet I knew roughly where to put the box, so I crossed the room.

I got halfway. My feet caught something on the floor, like a piece of furniture, firm and unmovable, and I tripped. The box hit the floor with a thud, followed by a loud clatter of empty bottles rolling out as I landed on my hands and knees in the dark.

"Hey, Bernie—you all right?" Nat called out, and then I heard a *click*—apparently the light switch—and the overhead fluorescent tubes flickered to life. Bright light dispelled the darkness, and I had to blink to adjust to it.

The first thing I saw was Anne's briefcase on the floor. A hairpin was jammed into the lock, and there were scratches all around, as if someone had tried, unsuccessfully, to open it.

Then I heard Nino curse and Roberto mutter half a prayer, and I turned to look back at what I'd stumbled over.

It was Anne. She lay still.

"Quick, we need to get help," I said, as I scrambled to my feet.

Nat was the first out the door, then I followed, and the two others behind me.

As Nat was announcing what had happened, I reached Phil and whispered, "Make sure all doors are locked and no one can get out."

His eyes widened with shock, but he nodded.

Then chaos erupted.

"Murder!" Mrs. Viola cried out, her voice rising to a hysterical pitch.

Peewee cursed, pushing people out of his way. "I need to see her—where is she?"

"I've got Chief Tedesco on the line," Angelica said.

"Where's my husband?" Gina wailed. "Where is Roberto?!"

"I'm right here."

"Thank God." She rushed at him and clung to him, arms wrapped tight. "I thought maybe ..."

Phil checked the front door was locked. Then headed for the office, and I went with him.

He checked that the office back door was locked.

"It was open," Phil said. "But it's locked now."

He backed out of the office, exhibiting a perfectly normal squeamishness at seeing a corpse. I'd hate to say it, but I was beginning to get used to it.

Nat came into the room and joined me. The two of us stood over Anne's dead body.

She was lying on her side, her face contorted in death. Her neck bore the marks of scratching and, most shockingly, a deep groove across. She'd apparently been strangled—my guess was with some kind of rope or wire.

"Something's wrong."

"You don't say," Nat said. "While we were drinking wine and talking books, Anne Adams was being murdered back here."

"No, Nat. I mean, about her briefcase."

He grabbed my arm, shocked. "Hey, you're right."

We looked at each other.

"It's gone," I said.

**2**

---

"Another pignoli cookie?" Angelica asked, putting a second tray on the table in Moroni's.

Chief Tedesco nodded her thanks and munched on another cookie. As Officers Ferrante and Fontana secured the scene of the crime, she'd brought everyone to the cafe down the street to take their statements.

Now she and I sat at a table together.

It had been a long night. We'd gone through a lot of *caffe longos*, *lattes*, and *espressos*, not to mention heaps of cookies. Angelica made sure no one's blood sugar got low.

"This is a nasty case," Tedesco said.

She sighed, either because she was tired or because Angelica's pignoli cookies often made people sigh with pleasure. She ran a hand across her eyes. Her bowl haircut, I noticed, had more streaks of gray in it than before. I didn't envy her job.

She glanced over one shoulder, then the other, checking on the others in the cafe—Nat and Peewee sat at a nearby table—before leaning toward me.

"Mrs. Viola told me several items vanished from the historical society's display. A few old photographs and—"

"Don't tell me," I said. "The garrote wire."

Tedesco nodded. "The killer apparently stole it and then used it to kill Anne Adams."

I held up my hands and pressed them against my ears. "No more. I don't want to hear this. I promised Angelica—heck, I promised myself—that I would devote myself fully to Moroni's. We've got the semi-finals for Carmine's Junior Baking Competition coming up."

Since leaving Milano Books, I'd had plenty of time to think this whole thing through. Nat might be right about my insatiable curiosity. My old investigating muscles—first toned in my days as Eve Silver, TV detective extraordinaire —did itch to be exercised. And Anne's murder was tragic. She deserved justice. But apart from finding her body, I had nothing to do with her death.

"I can't," I said. "Not this time."

"Bernie ..." Tedesco gently removed my hands, one by one, from my ears. "I understand. And I wouldn't ask for your help if I didn't—"

"Did someone say they needed help?"

Chief Tedesco stiffened. She dropped her hands to her lap.

Peewee, appearing next to our table, smiled down at us as he adjusted his glasses. "I'll help. I can't just sit around." He pulled out a chair and sat down. "Not while a murderer runs free. I've got to do something for Anne, or I'll feel worthless. Plus, I'm a bit of an amateur sleuth."

"I thought you only wrote mafia thrillers," I said. "Not whodunnits."

"Oh, I can write anything. Besides, I've got experience working with the FBI. In fact, I bet they'd be interested in a murder like this one—I mean, it's got 'mafia' written all over it. But maybe we'd better get some leads before we contact the FBI."

Tedesco clapped her hands together. "Mr. Puglisi, what a great idea! Why don't you and Bernie do some careful asking around town to see if you can sniff out any clues? But anything you learn, you report back to me, *capisce*?"

Peewee nodded enthusiastically. "You got it."

"I don't know ..." I said.

Tedesco grabbed my hand and squeezed it. "You'd be doing me a favor, Bernie."

Something in her look told me she wasn't just asking. She was begging.

"Oh," I said, letting out a long sigh. "All right, then."

~

The next day, Sunday, Peewee welcomed Nat and me to his house on Cedar Hill in the morning. Cedar Hill was where Carmine's wealthiest people lived, and Peewee's Victorian mansion must've cost more than one book advance.

The house was an ostentatious mix of architectural styles, including Queen Anne and Italianate. It looked like a mash-up between a giant wedding cake and the Addams Family home. The four-storied house had stained glass windows, a wraparound porch, and intricate woodwork, reaching into a massive tower at the center.

He must've guessed what we were thinking, because, as he escorted us from the front door down a massive hallway, he said, "Impressive, isn't it? When I taught English at Carmine High, I could barely afford an apartment on the other side of Garibaldi Avenue, and now, thanks to my series recently being optioned for a TV series, I live in a mansion."

The ballroom-sized living room was tastefully decorated, with a mix of modern furniture and antiques, including Tiffany lamps. Plus original art on the walls. At one end stood a giant oak desk with a fountain pen stand and one of those desk globes that sometimes hide a bottle of whiskey.

Behind the desk, tall, built-in shelves were crammed with hardbound and paperback books. Many of the spines were identical, and as Nat perused the books, he pointed out the many copies of Peewee's own Frankie F. series.

"I've read them all. My favorite is *Death Comes to Those Who Wait.* I can't wait to read the new one."

"Grab a copy," Peewee said. "I've got plenty."

Nat grinned as he reached up the shelf and grabbed one of the many copies of *Sicilians Wear Black,* the new Frankie F. thriller, then joined us by a set of sofas, clutching the book in his hands, with the excitement of a kid being given a bag of his favorite candy.

"I invited Nino to join us," Peewee said, as we got comfortable in sofas arranged around a coffee table. "But he declined. He's not as enthusiastic about sleuthing as I am. Or people." He chuckled. "If Nino had his way, he'd spend his days communing with books, and only books."

A coffee press and three cups sat on a tray. Peewee served us both before pouring for himself.

In front of us, a long bank of windows and a set of glass doors led to an outdoor patio and a long, sloping backyard. The patio glistened with newly fallen rain. Flecks of water dappled the windows. But the sun was emerging from behind the clouds.

"How did the two of you meet?" I asked.

"Nino and me? He moved to Carmine—let's see ..." He scratched his chin. "It must've been 10 years ago. Maybe a little less. I'd written a few books, nothing successful, and felt it was time to get serious. My books are research intensive, so I knew I needed help. I asked around. Luckily, Nino had arrived recently and needed work."

"And what about Anne?"

"Poor Anne." He shook his head. "She wasn't my first agent. When I got serious about my writing, I ditched my old agent and signed with Anne based on the strength of my first Frankie F. book."

"She's from Carmine originally?"

"When she was married to Roberto, they lived in the area and she commuted into the city. But she was born in Hoboken, and if you'd asked her, she'd say Manhattan was home. She hated Carmine."

"Because of what happened to her marriage?"

"She hated it while she lived here." He sighed. "Anne hated a lot of things. Deep down, she wasn't a happy person. And I sensed her unhappiness had gotten worse lately—it was affecting her work."

He took a sip of coffee and seemed to consider whether to speak or not. Then, making a decision, he put down his cup and said, "Look, let me be honest. She was becoming a problem. I was going to fire her."

This didn't surprise me. The way Peewee had been talking to Nino about Anne in Phil back-room office suggested their relationship was on the rocks.

"Did she know how unhappy you were with her?"

"Probably," Peewee said. "I think she could see the writing on the wall, and maybe that was why her behavior got even worse. You saw how she acted at the book event."

I nodded. "About her briefcase. She was guarding it, as if

it contained important documents. And then she said something about—"

"A napkin," Nat said.

"Yes," Peewee smiled. "A napkin. She was comparing my scribbles on a napkin to my latest manuscript. I assume she had a copy in the briefcase. She also had a copy of my book tour itinerary. Officially, it doesn't kick off until next month. I'm doing New York City, Boston, Atlanta, Memphis, Miami, Chicago, San Francisco, Los Angeles, and Seattle. Milano Books was like an appetizer."

"Anything else in the briefcase?"

He shrugged. "What do I know? Usually, she'd keep a legal pad and a pen for meetings. But honestly, I don't see how any of it could be valuable to anyone—not valuable enough to kill for."

"What about original manuscripts," Nat asked, "wouldn't they be worth something at auction?"

"Maybe when I'm dead. But we thriller writers need a long and illustrious career before collectors and academics take any interest in our sophomoric sketches and errata. No, the briefcase going missing makes no sense. Maybe it was done deliberately, you know, to throw us off the scent."

I didn't agree or disagree. The contents did seem innocent enough, but I'd seen evidence of someone trying to break open the briefcase before it went missing. The killer must've been spooked by someone, abandoned the effort, and then—what?—found a way to whisk the briefcase away later. But why?

Peewee must've noticed my look of concentration, because he laughed. "You're so focused on that briefcase, you're not seeing the elephant in the room."

"What elephant?"

"The garrote wire."

"The missing murder weapon."

"Right. Take a look at this ..." He got up and went to the desk, opening a drawer and pulling out a sheet of paper. "Nino handles my fan mail. Imagine his surprise when, the other day, we got this."

It was a photocopy of a letter, one of those crude ransom notes pasted together with cutout letters from newspaper headlines. Only it wasn't a ransom note. It was a death threat.

U talk 2 much. I going 2 break U fingers N shut U mouth 4 U. So U never talk no more.

I passed the note to Nat, who gave a low whistle.

"This is a copy," Peewee explained. "I gave the original to the police, of course. They've got other death threats. You'd be surprised how many I receive."

"Any idea who sent this one?" I asked.

"In fact, the cops are pretty sure it's a former mobster named Manny Manzo. He's the inspiration for Vinnie Albanese in my previous two books—and the most recent one."

"Which is Vinnie's last," Nat said. "Frankie finally kills him."

Peewee nodded. "Apparently, Manny reads my books, and he's none too thrilled about the similarities between Vinnie and himself. And the fact that I kill him off in *Sicilians Wear Black*."

"But what's this got to do with Anne's death?"

"Well, what if Manny tried to get to me? He learns about the event. A great place for an assassination, because there are so many suspects and so much DNA contamination. He finds the back door to Milano Books unlocked, sneaks in, but then Anne is resting on the couch. She wakes and is about to raise the alarm."

"So he kills her," Nat said. "Then flees when someone else comes along."

"But what makes you think it was Manny, specifically, who came to kill you. You said you get a lot of these death threats."

"Because of Manny's preferred method of murder—it's seriously old school."

"Garotting."

Peewee nodded. "He's the best in the business."

## 3

The sun stood high in the sky, only a few clouds remaining. Still, the grass in Puccini Park was damp. I'd used a tissue to wipe off the park bench before sitting down.

After leaving Peewee's home, Nat and I had parted ways. He had plans with his uncle. I stopped by Martini's Italian Market and bought a mortadella sandwich, which I only ate half of, and then proceeded to tear it apart and feed it to the park pigeons.

I had attracted a whole congregation of birds when someone sat down next to me on the bench.

It was Father Bruno, Carmine's parish priest. St. Joseph's Catholic Church sat at one end of Puccini Park, so in a way, this was his backyard.

He was a quiet, soft-spoken man with large brown eyes and unusually long lashes, reminding me of a doe-eyed deer.

He said, "You know, you shouldn't do that."

"I know. Feed a pigeon, breed a rat."

"No, that's not what I meant. I meant bottle up emotions.

I can see what's eating the bread—" He stamped his feet, sending the birds fluttering away. "—but what's eating you?"

"It's nothing."

"I talk to people about 'nothing' every day. Allow me to butcher Shakespeare: Nothing good will come of saying nothing, so speak again."

I glanced at him. His big doe eyes were regarding me calmly, patiently. I had the absurd idea that if I sat on this bench for a hundred years, he'd wait by my side until I opened up.

"All right," I said. "I feel I'm letting someone down."

"Angelica?"

I narrowed my eyes. "How did you know?"

"Elementary, my dear Bernie. She's the most likely candidate for guilt given that she's your friend, you work for her, and you've often been pulled away from your work by —" He paused. "—other responsibilities."

"But that's the problem. They're not my responsibilities. Chief Tedesco is responsible for investigating murders. And yet whenever some crime is committed, I can't help it—I get pulled in."

"Pulled or pushed? Sometimes we feel the tug, and although we could resist, we give ourselves a little kick in the *culo*. And that's what sends us flying."

I shoved the rest of my sandwich in the brown paper bag from Martini's, and then leaned forward, elbows on my knees, head in my hands.

"I should be the best bakery assistant and barista in the world. Angelica deserves a reliable employee. But instead, I'm off playing amateur detective. I should tell everyone once and for all what my real job is."

"You mean *actress*?"

"No." I looked up at Father Bruno. "Of course not."

"But that's who you were for many years."

"I was ..." I shook my head. "But then I wasn't ..."

"And yet people continue to see you as a famous actress, or even as your character, Eve Silver, don't they?"

I nodded.

"Is that who you are?"

I shook my head.

"Very well, Bernie. Let me tell you a story about a parishioner of mine. A guy named—let's call him DeGrazio. He used to work for the mafia. But over time, he saw the evil he was doing. Now, you and I can discuss how a man can do evil for years and not see the bad in it, and then I would tell you the story of Paul the Apostle, who spent years persecuting Christians before seeing the light on the road to Damascus. But this isn't a sermon."

Father Bruno smiled his shy smile.

"So, back to the story. My parishioner decides to leave the mafia. But what is he to do? His whole life he's been trained to cheat and hurt. He recalls his old friends and envies them for their ignorance—after all, there was a time when he believed what they believed, and thought himself happy. Or if not happy, then in the right place. With a clear purpose. He looks around at his new neighbors. They are doctors and nurses and school teachers. People who do good. And he envies them even more. For they took a righteous path. He knew that he would never be a doctor or nurse or school teacher. So what was left for him?"

Father Bruno stared out at Puccini Park. The green grass. The sycamore trees. The white bandstand. I followed his gaze, then turned back to him, waiting for the rest of the story.

"Well?" I asked.

"Well," he said. "As St. Augustine says, 'Men go abroad to

admire the heights of mountains, the mighty waves of the sea, the broad tides of rivers, the compass of the ocean, and the circuits of the stars, yet pass over the mystery of themselves without a thought.' There are always more than two paths, in spite of what Robert Frost might say in that poem of his."

"So which path did this guy take?"

"Does it matter, Bernie? Does it matter which path this guy took—or the path I've taken—or the path your friends Nat and Angelica have taken? The path they've chosen won't tell you which you should take."

"But I have chosen," I said. "I've accepted the job at Moroni's, and that means I have a responsibility to Angelica."

"To show up in the morning, yes. To ask her permission if you leave work early, yes. But to devote your life to the bakery?" He shook his head. "You worry about what Angelica might think when you are absent for a few hours. What would she think if you were permanently absent? If you left Moroni's?"

He raised his eyebrows and stared at me.

The mere idea of ever leaving Moroni's made my stomach twist into a terrible knot.

"But I don't want to leave Angelica."

"That's not what I said. I said Moroni's."

"But Angelica—"

I cut myself off. I forced myself to think of Angelica and Moroni's as separate entities. I couldn't. I couldn't even separate them from all of Carmine.

"Do you judge Nat or Angelica for their choices, Bernie? No, I imagine you don't. And they won't judge you. They'll be happy to see you on the right path. The question is, What's the right path for you?"

I felt sick to my stomach. My head was a whirl of disjointed thoughts, inducing a kind of vertigo. I'd rather turn away than look at that swirling mess.

*Yes, forget what Father Bruno said. Leave Moroni's? He must be crazy. It can never happen.*

We sat in silence for a long time.

"Think about it," Father Bruno said. "But don't *worry* about it. The answer will come to you—and probably when you least expect it. Now, I'm afraid I have to go." He looked at his wristwatch. "I have afternoon Mass, and given the path I've chosen, I better not be late." He smiled. "In fact, I don't want to be late."

We said our goodbyes.

The birds pecked at my feet. I stared out at the park, trying to still my beating heart.

**4**

———

Monday morning, Angelica was showing me the decorations she'd ordered for the upcoming competition. It wasn't a big event, especially since only the tasting and judging, not the baking, were live. There were pennants that would be strung across the bakery. The diplomas for the three top winners—first, second, and third place—with spaces for names. And even t-shirts that said, "Carmine's Junior Baking Competition," alongside the name of the bakery and the event sponsor.

"Grande's Baking Emporium," I read off the t-shirt. "Isn't that owned by that guy on TV who calls himself the Prince of the Patisserie? That's a big sponsor for such a small event."

"Michael Grande's his name. He's from Carmine originally."

"Ah, hometown connections."

"They're the best," Angelica said with a big smile.

She folded the t-shirt and put it back in the box that sat on the counter, then carried it into her office out back.

While she was gone, I leaned against the display counter, appreciating the coziness of Moroni's.

Morning light shone on the tiled floor. The display was packed with cookies and other mouth-watering Italian baked goods. The air was heavy with the sweet scent of baking and the rich aroma of freshly brewed coffee.

And yet my mind kept drifting to Manny Manzo. I'd called Chief Tedesco last night to inform her, and she'd thanked me.

"The idea that we're looking for an out-of-towner fits with the evidence so far," she said. "But I don't know about this Manzo character. I'm pursuing a lead on a thriller writer who used to be Anne Adams's client—they had a falling out. Interestingly, he came to the event."

I considered this new information, remembering the drunk thriller writer who had accidentally walked into the office rather than the restroom. Or so he said.

I was still mulling this over when the door to Moroni's opened, making the little bell jingle.

Lily, one of the baking competition semi-finalists, entered with a big, sunny smile. She wore black lace-up boots, jeans, and a black t-shirt advertising a band called "Amon Amarth."

"I'm guessing Amon Amarth has nothing to do with the ancient grain amaranth."

Lily laughed. "Swedish death metal isn't your thing, is it Bernie?"

I shook my head. But who was I to judge? For all her black nail polish and piercings, Lily never looked glum. Maybe Swedish death metal was the ticket to happiness. Maybe. I planned to stick to Louis Prima for now.

Angelica returned from the back of the bakery.

Digging into a knapsack, Lily pulled out her notebook—which never left her side—and got a pencil ready.

"So, Angelica," she said. "I was thinking, if I do a raspberry-infused chocolate soufflé, how would I best combine the chocolate and raspberry infusion?"

Angelica smiled. "Since I'm judging the competition later this week, do you think I should answer that question?"

Lily frowned. After a moment of quiet contemplation, she said, "You're right. I shouldn't have asked. I guess I'm so excited, and I usually ask you like a million questions, so I thought, you know, whatever." Then she shoved her pencil and notebook back into her bag. "I want to win because my cake is the best, not because I got help."

I admired Lily, not only for her commitment to baking, but also for her integrity. Since I'd met her, she'd proven to be a serious, hardworking teen with a solid set of values. I didn't doubt she'd go far in life.

If anyone deserved to win the baking competition, it was Lily.

Lily sighed. "I usually bring my samples for you to taste, Angelica. And I get it, I can't do that. Not with you judging the competition. But none of my family members or friends are interested ..."

"I'll help," I said.

"You will?"

"Sure. I can be your guinea pig. And you can use my kitchen to practice." I turned to Angelica. "We're not breaking any rules by doing that, are we?"

Angelica smiled. "You're only being a good friend."

Lily and I agreed to meet after work at my place on Wednesday, so Lily could use my kitchen and serve me some samples.

Lily grinned. "Great! Thanks, Bernie."

She checked the time on her cell phone—"Oops, gotta go!"—and rushed out, nearly colliding with Roberto Rizzoli as he entered Moroni's. Behind him came Gina and, to my surprise, Mrs. Greco.

I had met Mrs. Greco on a previous case, when her son, Johnny, had been killed. She lived in a fancy old Victorian house on Cedar Hill, where she'd spent many years secluded from the world. Since breaking free from her sheltered life, she now played an active role in the Carmine community.

She greeted Angelica and me warmly. Roberto, his face sagging with lack of sleep, added a polite hello. And the two of them perused the display. Gina gave a nod, didn't make eye contact, and hurried to a table. When she pulled out a chair, it screeched, and the sound made her jump.

"Guess the murder must have rattled her," I whispered to Angelica.

"Both of them," Angelica said. "But that's hardly surprising. Roberto and Anne might've parted on bad terms, but they were still married for years."

I made cappuccinos for all three. Mrs. Greco ordered three slices of Angelica's chocolate walnut cake and then sprang from her seat when Roberto insisted on paying. She reached the counter before he could get out of his chair—and swiped her credit card, paying for coffee and cake.

"It's the least I can do," she told me. "Roberto is a saint. He's come all this way from Seattle to help his mother move into assisted care. You couldn't ask for a better son."

The words had extra significance coming from Mrs. Greco. No one had expected her own son, Johnny, to be canonized by the Vatican.

I cut three generous slices of the chocolate walnut cake

and brought them to the table.

Roberto said, "My mom has reached the age where she can no longer drive—or even handle the stairs in her house. She was lucky to get an apartment at Lakeview Assisted Care Facility. It's a big move. So Gina and I came back to help her with the move."

"Well, Roberto came back," Gina said. "And I had a chance to see Carmine for myself."

"Your first time here?" I asked.

She nodded. "We flew in on Friday and got Primo's Taxi to pick us up. My home state is California, but we live in Seattle."

"No desire to move to Carmine?"

Gina glanced at Roberto. "It's a charming town, but our lives are out west."

"I have enough memories from Carmine," he said. "A lifetime's worth."

I noticed he didn't say whether they were good memories or bad. But he gave me a meaningful look as if we both knew he was alluding to his marriage with Anne.

"I'm sorry for your loss," I said.

"Thank you. In truth, Anne and I hadn't talked in years. If we hadn't come to Carmine to see my mom, I doubt she and I would've reconnected. I did reach out to her, but she refused to engage."

"You mean you contacted her before you saw her at Milano Books?"

"Several times. God asks us to be kind and tender-hearted to one another. I wished for us to reconcile."

Gina added, "If you do not forgive others their sins, your Father will not forgive your sins."

At times, Roberto and Gina sounded as if they were warming up to deliver a sermon.

"Wait, what sins had Anne committed?"

"She committed a mortal sin," Roberto said, "by breaking one of the 10 Commandments."

Gina said, "*You shall not commit adultery.*"

Confused, I looked to Mrs. Greco, and she simply shrugged.

"I thought ..."

"... that I cheated on Anne with Gina?" Roberto said. "No. She liked everyone to think that. She liked to think that everything that went wrong was a direct attack on her—and somehow everyone else was to blame. But the fact is that I caught her cheating with a younger man right here in Carmine."

"Is he still here?"

"I saw him the other day. He's a police officer."

Bernie groaned. "Not Anthony Ferrante ..."

~

At the end of the work day, I helped Angelica clean up and lock up Moroni's. I'd promised myself to focus on my bakery work, but Anthony Ferrante and I had history, and I wanted to hear straight from the horse's mouth what his involvement with Anne Adams had been.

I called Nat and arranged to meet him at his work, so we could both go to the Old Mill, Carmine's local watering hole. Our chances of meeting said horse there was high.

When I stepped inside the Carmine Public Library, Nat was waiting for me at the circulation desk.

"An informant has told me that Anthony's planning to go for a drink tonight with Fontana," he told me with a wink. "Well, Jerry told me."

Jerry was the bartender at the Old Mill, and as reliable source as you could get. To kill time, I asked Nat if he wanted to show me the rest of the historical society's collection.

"I thought you'd never ask," he said, as he led me through the library to a room at the back. A sign over the door said, Carmine Historical Appreciation & Preservation Society.

I was a little embarrassed to be stepping over the threshold for the first time. Nat and I had been friends since my first couple of weeks in Carmine, and although I had dropped in on him at the public library, I'd never come to see the work he did at the historical society.

The room devoted to Carmine's history was tiny. No more than 20 feet long and wide. Display cases ringed the walls. In the center stood a long table with library books on display as well as stands with placards providing historical timelines and descriptions of Carmine through the ages.

Nat showed me one of the display cases.

"This one documents the history of the old sawmill."

Black-and-white photographs showed men in overalls with hats, the brims turned up to reveal suspicious glares. In the background a team of horses was loaded with timber.

"And here's one much later," he pointed out. "The year before they closed the mill."

"They look less suspicious."

"They probably weren't as uncomfortable with the camera. Photography had become more—" He gave me a nudge. "—run of the mill."

There were lots more photographs. Of Independence Day parades in the 1950s, a tiny war protest in the late '60s —a half a dozen hippies on the steps of town hall—and then a grim photo of a girl in handcuffs flanked by two doughy cops. The caption simply said, Rita Glen, with a date 20 years ago. There was a newspaper clipping next to it: "Carmine teenager kills classmate; police suspect foul play."

"Wow," I said. "I didn't know about this story."

I was impressed by the range of items and how well curated they were. Mrs. Viola hadn't made a good impression on me. But she must have some strong investigation skills to unearth all these stories and put them together in a way that made sense.

When I shared my thoughts with Nat, I was surprised to hear him praise Mrs. Viola.

"Yeah, she's a rock star."

"A rock star? She seemed so—"

"Sure, she can be a pain, but you should see her track down information. She'd make Eve Silver proud. Oh, take a look at this one."

Nat pointed to another newspaper clipping. This one had a photo of Moroni's Italian Bakery, and out front was a much younger Angelica—no silver streak in her hair—handing a trophy to a young man with a big smile. The caption said, "Carmine youth, Michael Grande, wins first prize in baking competition."

"Well, what do you know," I said. "The Prince of the Patisserie."

"There's so much media stuff about him we could fill the whole room with photos and articles. We've stopped at this news article and a magazine profile from when he really got big."

Nat pointed at a cutout from a glossy magazine. The article mentioned Michael Grande's trademark passion fruit cake with its thin wafer base—signed with a distinctive swirl of chocolate—and his bestselling chocolate gateau, which had almost single-handedly given rise to Grande's Baking Emporium during the last decade's "Choco Gateau Craze."

"I didn't even know there was such a thing as a Choco Gateau Craze," I said.

Nat tsk-tsked. "You heathens in the entertainment industry were so out of touch."

I gave him a playful shove.

"Oh," he said, and led me to the next display, "take a look at these."

But just then, Mrs. Viola strode into the room, a finger aimed at Nat as if it were the barrel of a gun.

"You," she said. "Where's my garrote wire?"

"Your garrote wire?" Nat's bangs were obstructing his glasses. He swept them to the side. "Presumably, the killer's taking good care of it."

"Don't get fresh with me, young man."

"If I knew where the murder weapon was, Mrs. Viola, I'd tell Chief Tedesco. I'm sure she'd like to know."

"Chief Tedesco." Mrs. Viola let out a loud breath, an expression that suggested she had little confidence in the Carmine police department. "If she had any sense, she'd take a close look at that Gina woman."

I perked up my ears. "Why do you say that, Mrs. Viola? Is there something suspicious about the Rizzolis?"

"Roberto Rizzoli, suspicious? My goodness, no. Roberto's an angel." She narrowed her eyes. "But he's always been the victim of venomous women. Look at that Anne. She was a viper. And that Gina isn't what she pretends to be, any fool can see that." She seemed to realize the implication of what she was saying. "But my Roberto, he's no fool, of course. Deep down, he knows. Mark my words, that relationship won't last, and when it ends, Roberto will find the person he was always meant to be with—his soulmate."

She got a faraway look in her eyes.

Nat and I exchanged glances.

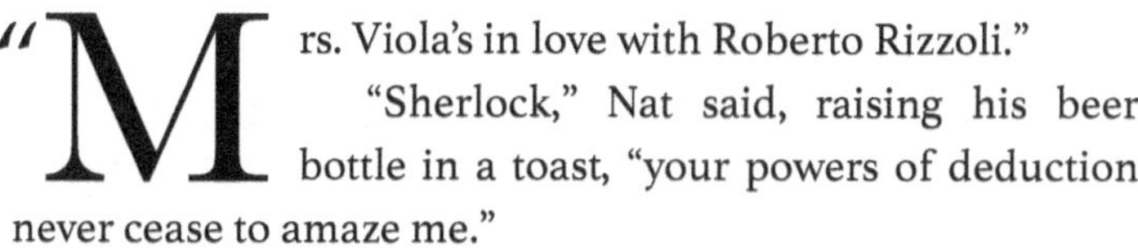

"**M**rs. Viola's in love with Roberto Rizzoli."

"Sherlock," Nat said, raising his beer bottle in a toast, "your powers of deduction never cease to amaze me."

We were sitting at the bar in the Old Mill. Long ago, the place had been the town sawmill, center of the Carmine economy, as the historical society explained so well. Today, it was the best—actually, the only—bar in town. And technically, it wasn't even in town—it was nestled along the wooded road to Lake Carmine.

Exposed wooden beams cut across the ceiling. Wide floorboards stretched under the few tables and booths. The long, hardwood bar gleamed. A stuffed deer head jutted out of a wall, antlers and all, and below it stood an old jukebox. Often, the music featured crooners, but right now it was playing country music: Rose Maddox's "I'm Happy Everyday I Live."

Nat assured me that Rose Maddox was part Italian—no doubt why Jerry, the bartender, played her music.

I steered the conversation back to our main topic: "When did you find out?"

"About Rose Maddox?"

"No, silly. About Mrs. Viola's obsession with Roberto Rizzoli?"

"Oh, on day one of my job. She'll sit at that desk of hers and mutter his name without realizing it: '*Roberto, Roberto, Rob.*'"

"Sounds kind of sad." I took a swig of beer and considered the idea of Mrs. Viola and Roberto Rizzoli. "Isn't she a lot older than him?"

"Bernie, Bernie, what does age matter when it comes to love? Besides, isn't that sexist? Or ageist? Would you judge Roberto if he were with a younger woman?"

"I wouldn't dare judge him. He's too saintly."

"Anyway, they're actually about the same age. Mrs. Viola does herself no favors with how she dresses and acts. She must buy her outfits second hand from that headmistress in *Matilda*."

"Miss Trunchbull?"

"That's the one." Nat looked thoughtful. "She married a guy—"

"Mr. Viola, I presume."

"See, there you go again, Sherlock. But seriously, Mr. Viola died young. Or rather, Mrs. Viola married an older man who died at an age that isn't young or old."

"Don't tell me he was garroted ..."

Nat shook his head. "Heart attack. So if you're thinking of painting Mrs. Viola as a serial killer, don't bother."

My phone rang, and I dug it out of my pocket. My lock screen said, "Marco Puglisi."

I placed it on the table and let it ring.

Nat glanced at the screen. "You're ignoring Peewee Puglisi?"

I sighed.

"Say no more," Nat said.

"The guy calls me all the time. Leaves voice messages with ideas for how to 'pursue the investigation,' as he says. I'm beginning to think Chief Tedesco pawned him off on me. I'm not investigating—I'm babysitting."

"Puglisi?" Jerry said.

A bearded guy, Jerry was never out of a flannel shirt, and

rarely spoke more than a few syllables at a time. Tonight was no different. He reached under the counter and brought up a copy of Peewee's latest Frankie F. novel and gave us a thumbs up.

"You're a fan, too?" I asked. "Is there anyone in this town who isn't a Puglisi fan?"

"Not me—I haven't read his books." Anthony Ferrante, as handsome as ever, joined us at the bar. "I'm waiting for them to make a TV show."

*Because a book is hard work,* I thought. But I wasn't going to get snarky with Anthony. I could do that anytime I wanted, and I felt entitled to do it, too, after the way he'd given me the runaround. Tonight, I needed to be on good behavior. I needed answers.

"Anthony," I said. "You must be exhausted. What with this investigation and—"

"Cut it out, Bernie." He eyed me wearily, as if he were, in fact, exhausted. He pointed to a tap and Jerry served him a pint of beer. "I know why you're hanging out here and what you're doing. Jerry told you I was stopping by."

Nat chuckled. "He out-sleuthed the sleuth."

Anthony shrugged. "Jerry told you. Then he told me."

I looked at Jerry and frowned. "Jerry, you talk too much."

Jerry, silent as usual, gave me a shrug and continued wiping down the bar.

"All right," I said, getting straight to the point. "Anne Adams and you."

Anthony grimaced and tried to hide his embarrassment by drinking. But the pint glass wasn't big enough for him to hide in, and eventually he had to come up for air.

"So it's true," I said.

He nodded.

"And you had the affair while she was married to Roberto?"

He nodded again, his shoulders slumping. He seemed to be shrinking.

"I was just having fun," he said, and his own ears must've told him how bad that excuse sounded because they turned bright red. So he changed tack. "Honestly, it was awful. As soon as it started, I wanted out. She was mean. She kept saying nasty things about her husband, Roberto, who actually seems like a decent guy."

"Yeah, you must've really respected him."

"You've got to believe me, Bernie. I was the one being used."

"How do you figure that?"

"Listen, the times we met, it was always at her house, and each time, I had to get out fast, because her husband came home unexpectedly. Only I don't think it was unexpected."

"You think she planned it that way? Why, for the extra thrill?"

"When he finally did find out," Anthony said, and swallowed another gulp of beer to steady himself. "It was over."

"What, their marriage or your affair?"

"Both."

I ran a hand over my face. "All right, Anthony. I thought I'd never say this, but you're too subtle for me. Why don't you spell it out for me? Because I'm not getting it."

"Don't you see? She wanted Roberto to catch us. She wanted the marriage to break up. And when it did, she was done with me—she dropped me like a hot potato."

"But why would she do that? Why not just leave him?"

"She hated him," Anthony said. "And she said he hated her, too."

Nat left the Old Mill early. Mrs. Viola had demanded he show up early to redo the categorization of the Carmine Italian Day Celebration photographs from 1970 to 2000. I stayed for another drink at the bar. The Monday night crowd, already rail thin, was thinning out even more.

At the bar, there was only Jerry and me—and sitting on a stool and nursing a seltzer, Primo Leone, the taxi driver.

I enjoyed the quiet, welcoming a little alone time to reflect on what I'd learned.

Anne had pretended that Roberto had cheated on her, when in fact she was the one who'd had an affair. And she'd done it deliberately to break up the marriage—and to hurt Roberto.

Jerry was wiping down the bar again. If he made it any cleaner, it could double as a mirror.

"Hey, Jerry, why do you think Anne would use Anthony to break up her own marriage? If she hated Roberto Rizzoli so much, why not just divorce him?"

Jerry kept running the cloth back and forth.

"Good Christian," he said.

"She hardly behaved like one."

He shook his head. "No, Roberto."

I considered that for a moment. "Because he's a good Catholic?"

Primo Leone, from down the bar, said, "Nah, Roberto Rizzoli left the Catholic Church years ago. He's one of them born-again Christians. Happy to tell you all about it, too. I drove him and his wife from the airport, and the guy sure knows how to talk. When it comes to religion, the guy's a real *giacchieron'*." Primo looked at me. "A blabbermouth, you know?"

"I still don't get it. Why did Anne need to have an affair to end the marriage?"

"See, I figure it went down like this. Roberto got born again during their marriage. That's a fact. I'm gonna guess Anne wasn't so happy about it, but when she says she wants to divorce Rob, he says no. That kinda thing isn't acceptable."

"But adultery is?"

Primo shrugged. "It's complicated. There's a whole thing in the Bible about divorce and adultery, and even Father Bruno can't give me a straight answer. See, it's in Matthew. It says something like if a guy divorces his wife, and then he marries again, he's committing adultery. Unless she's two-timing him. Then the guy's got the green light to move on."

"Jeez, you know a lot about this, Primo."

"I know a lot about everything. I listen to people, and people love to talk to cab drivers. It's a fact."

He had a point. Taxi drivers and hairdressers were the original Wikipedia, with half the world filling them with random facts—some true, and others not so true.

"Plus, I've got this regular client," Primo said. "He's a church-going divorce lawyer. He's got a lot to say on the topic."

"OK," I said. "So Roberto doesn't see unhappiness as grounds for divorce, but adultery is the exception."

"You got it. See, Father Bruno wouldn't give an annulment because of adultery, but that's the Catholic side of things. Rob, he's part of a Protestant church, so he's all right with it."

"All right with adultery?"

"All right with a divorce."

"Sounds awfully complicated."

Primo drained his seltzer and setting the empty glass on the bar, slipped off the stool. "Maybe Anne also enjoyed messing with Rob. She hated him, right? So Catholic or Protestant or Atheist or whatever, someone cheating on you makes you sad or mad."

He saluted Jerry, who gave Primo a nod.

The theology lesson had exhausted me. I pushed my half-empty beer across the counter, no longer wanting the rest. What I wanted was sleep. This case was a headache. In the morning, I would ignore the whole thing and devote myself entirely to Moroni's.

"Hey, Primo, you still on duty?"

"I'll drive you home, if that's what you're askin'."

A minute later, I was sitting in Primo's cab, and we were pulling out of the Old Mill's parking lot. It was late. The road was empty. As we rolled down the hill toward Garibaldi Avenue, I tried to stifle a yawn, and failed.

Primo said, "I hear you're working with Peewee Puglisi on this murder case."

"Where did you hear that?"

"People talk." He smiled. "Sounds great. I'd love to get inside that guy's head. I mean, how does he do it? His books are like a good Chianti—once you open it, you gotta finish it."

"You're a fan, too, huh?"

"He gets the details right. No messin' around with the facts."

"That's a big compliment coming from you."

"Because of my old job? That's all in the past. But it don't mean I don't think about it. And I got friends, you know, they're still connected."

This surprised me. Primo's job as a driver for the mafia

was decades in the past. My surprise must've shown, because Primo said, "I left on good terms. No hard feelings. So, once in a blue moon, some of my old friends still drop by and have a glass of sambuca. They tell me stuff."

We were cruising down Garibaldi Avenue, past Carlo's Restaurant, then Moroni's. The bakery's windows were dark, the red-checkered curtains looking black and white in the gloom. Overhead, the banner strung across the street that said, "*Benvenuti*—welcome!" shook in the evening breeze.

A little while later, Primo turned the car onto Da Vinci Street. Soon, we'd get to my home, and with the direction the conversation had taken, I knew Eve Silver wouldn't have hesitated to ask more questions. One in particular.

"Primo, you ever hear of a guy called Manny Manzo?"

"Mad Mouse Manzo. Sure. What about him?"

I told him about the death threat Peewee had shown me at his house.

Primo chuckled. "That's why he's called Mad Mouse. Guy's crazy. If he got any more paranoid, he'd think he was following himself."

Primo steered the car to the curb. We'd arrived at my little ranch-style home on Lampedusa Lane. I got out of the car, but kept the passenger door open and leaned in to keep the conversation going.

"So he's not a threat?"

"Even if he was, he ain't one any more."

"He's in jail?"

Primo shook his head. "Manny's sleeping with the fishes."

**5**

———

The next morning, I was helping Angelica string up pennants across the bakery cafe and hang posters advertising the Junior Baking Competition, when Nat came through the door.

"Aren't you supposed to be helping Mrs. Viola catalog photos?"

"She dismissed me," he said, and as I dropped the string of pennants I was holding, he quickly added, "Don't worry, she didn't fire me. But after I'd been working on the photos from 6 am this morning, she sent me away. Said she would have to do it all herself." He frowned. "My ego isn't easily bruised, but I'm beginning to feel that my talents aren't appreciated."

"Has she always been this way?"

"She's always seemed so—" He paused. "—in control. She's clearly worked up about something."

"When did it start? The night of the murder?"

"Maybe," he said. "No, wait. She was already upset on Friday."

I made espressos for Angelica, Nat, and myself as I

considered what had happened on Friday. It might be something in Mrs. Viola's life that had nothing to do with Anne's death.

I joined Nat at a table.

Then I remembered something.

"Gina Rizzoli said she and Roberto flew in on Friday and that Primo Leone picked them up at the airport. What if Mrs. Viola saw them when they got to Carmine?"

"That would make sense. She sees her beloved Rob with his new wife, and it digs up old wounds."

Nat dipped a biscotto into his espresso and munched it. Angelica joined us and for a while, we enjoyed our espressos and biscotti and talked. We talked about the upcoming competition, a new recipe for *panna cotta* that Angelica was trying out, and a funny story Nat told about the time the famous Italian opera singer Enrico Caruso visited Carmine and its old sawmill—I never thought I could laugh so hard at a story about opera arias and sawdust.

Moments like these were my happiest—when I had my best friends around me, and the sun was casting its golden light through Moroni's windows.

The front door opened, the bell jingled joyfully, and my heart sank.

"Morning," Peewee said, grinning that donkey grin of his.

"What can I get you?" Angelica asked.

"You can lend me your employee. Bernie, I want to swing by Nino's place and take a look at any suspicious fan mail that's come in. I'd like your help. What do say, partner?"

"I'd love to, Peewee. But Angelica and I are busy, we—"

"Don't worry, Bernie," Angelica cut in. "You can go."

"I really think I ought to stay and—"

"Great," Peewee said. "Are you coming too, Nat?"

Nat got to his feet. "Why not? If my talents are wanted, I'll be happy to join."

I sighed and finished the last morsel of biscotti.

Outside, Peewee had parked his car, a black SUV as big as a tank, no doubt compensation for his own diminutive size. I called shotgun, so Nat slipped into the back, and Peewee started the car and pulled onto Garibaldi Avenue.

He was playing Journey's Greatest Hits on the speakers. He drummed one hand against the steering wheel, proving that his talent was with words, not keeping rhythm.

"The threat from Manny Manzo made me think there might be more."

"You'll be happy to know that Manzo's not going to kill you." I told him what Primo had revealed, leaving out the cab driver's name. I said, "Last week, he had a boating accident down the shore. Nothing suspicious. Lots of witnesses saw him slip and fall and hit his head and then sink into the ocean. He's literally sleeping with the fishes. Or would be, if the body hadn't been recovered."

"Phew, what a relief," Peewee said. "I'd been worried about waking up and seeing Manzo's ugly face leaning over me. I only hope that means I was wrong about the mafia wanting to kill me. Nino has the latest fan mail—he'll know if anything suspicious has come in."

"Unless this murder is about something more personal," I suggested. "Something closer to home."

Peewee raised an eyebrow. "You mean, like a bitter ex-husband?"

"You know, at your book event, I thought I heard Anne say to Gina, 'He'll cheat again.'"

"But Anne was the one who cheated on Roberto, not the other way around."

"How do you know that?"

"Told you I was a bit of an amateur detective. Also, Anne was lousy at keeping secrets. Once she had something on her mind, she had to tell the whole world. You saw how she behaved on Saturday night."

"So she had a secret she wanted to reveal. What was it?"

"Who knows? It might not have been a secret. It might just have been Anne getting drunk and pouring out her venom. After all, her ex-husband had showed up with his new wife. That must have been a surprise. Here's Nino's house."

Up ahead lay a modest ranch-style house, very similar to my own, with a neatly trimmed front yard. Well, neater than my own, to be honest. Like golf course neat. Who has the patience to trim a lawn with nail clippers?

But I soon lost interest in the lawn. Because in the driveway stood a vehicle that I was all too familiar with. A USPS truck. It wasn't idling at the curb, as trucks delivering mail ought to. And if I'd been in doubt about who was driving it, she emerged from Nino's house at the very moment Peewee parked the SUV by the curb.

Roberta LaRosa.

"Looks like Nino's got a delivery—hopefully not more hate mail," Peewee said and chuckled, pushing his big glasses up his nose.

I said nothing. What could I say? That I knew that the United States Postal Service personnel didn't usually make house calls—they tended to hand over their packages at the door or leave them on the welcome mat. The U.S. Marshalls Service was a different story, though.

The USPS truck backed out and turned and then rumbled up the street, and I glanced at Peewee, trying to gauge if the incident had meant anything to him. But he seemed oblivious. He was turning off the car and getting out, cheerfully calling for Nat and me to follow.

Standing in Nino's driveway, I looked up the street and watched the USPS truck turn and disappear.

What was Roberta doing visiting Nino Clemenza?

Nino Clemenza's house smelled of sauce. After welcoming us in an apron, he gestured with a wooden spoon for us to go into the living room.

"Meatballs on the stove," he said.

"Smells like Carlo's Restaurant in here," I told Nat as we walked into the living room. And then forgot all about the food.

"Wow."

The living room was more like a library. Bookcases covered most of the walls. Where there wasn't room for cases, he'd mounted shelves. The back of the couch was a low, built-in bookshelf. The coffee table had space underneath, also crammed with books.

It ought to have been a recipe for chaos. But everything was neatly organized. In fact, taking a look at the shelves, I noticed the books were organized alphabetically by author and divided into sections, like a library.

"Incredible. He's organized his books according to the Dewey Decimal System," Nat said. He turned to Peewee, who was getting comfortable on the couch. "Hey, was Nino a librarian before he became your assistant?"

"That's right. He worked at a library."

At the far end of the living room, a desk stood against a wall. A desktop computer flashed its screensaver and there was a flip calendar and a book with a bookmark stuck into its pages. Otherwise the workspace was remarkably neat.

I noticed the squares on the flip calendar were almost all blank. There were a few entries that simply said, "Puglisi." And then one for today where the name or word had been crossed out. I couldn't make out what it had said.

On Saturday, at the bookstore, hadn't Nino mentioned something about a meeting with Anne being canceled?

Next to the desk, a doorway opened onto a short hallway at the end of which, I glimpsed Nino moving past a counter to open a fridge. Oddly, the counter was bare—no chopping board or discarded onion skin or other messy signs of cooking. My attempts at making sauce and meatballs usually left my kitchen looking like a bloodbath. But maybe I had a particular talent for making a mess.

I stepped down the hallway. A door to the right stood ajar and, careful not to make a sound, I pushed it open.

Inside was a bedroom.

There was a single bed against the wall. The covers were neatly tucked down the sides. Unlike the library-like living room, Nino's bedroom was bare. No photographs. No artwork. It reminded me of a monastic cell.

"I like tidy," Nino said, and I jumped, startled by his silent approach.

"It's nice," I said. "It reminds me of a friend I had who served in the Navy. We worked on a TV show. She couldn't kick her Navy habits. Did you serve in the military?"

"Not exactly."

"Peewee says you were a librarian."

"For a while, yeah."

He took a slight step toward me, and I found myself backing into the living room again. He did it subtly, without intimidating me (much), but he was definitely guiding me.

Again, under his apron, he was wearing a strangely formal outfit. No tie this time, but creased pants and a white shirt buttoned at the neck.

"You have an amazing collection of books," Nat said as Nino and I came into the living room.

"My one vice."

"I can think of worse ones."

Nino shrugged. "Maybe I order too many." He glanced at Peewee. "Mr. Puglisi, I just got another shipment of books on Sicilian history—you know, the ones we talked about."

"Ah," Peewee said. "Mystery solved. We were wondering about the USPS truck. See, Nino is researching the next Frankie F. book already, and it's going to touch on family history, going way back to the old country."

"I can't wait to read it," Nat said. He turned to Nino. "It must be amazing to do all this research and then see it take shape in Peewee's stories."

Nino nodded.

"After you do the research," I asked, "how much are you involved?"

"Nino does the fact checking," Peewee answered.

"Did you and Anne ever work together?"

Nino shook his head.

"And yet you knew each other," I said. "You took care of her on Saturday when she'd had too much to drink."

"I knew her," Nino agreed.

Peewee expanded on Nino's terse response: "Nino and Anne mostly knew each other from book signings and parties I've hosted at my home or at my publisher's in New York City. But they didn't collaborate on the editorial process." He smiled, showing his big teeth. "I spared Nino that torture, didn't I, Nino?"

"Yes, boss."

Then Peewee launched into an explanation of why we'd come, including a summary of my news about Manny Manzo. Nino received the news without any show of emotion.

"So," Peewee said. "Any other death threats come in?"

Nino crossed the room to his desk and opened a drawer and pulled out a piece of paper. He handed it to me.

Once again, it was a photocopy. This time the message had been written by hand in crude capital letters.


EXCEPT YE REPENT, YE SHALL LIKEWISE PERISH.


"Adapted from the Bible," Nino said. "Luke 13:3."

Peewee got to his feet and joined me, studying the paper. He sighed. "Probably just some religious nutcase. I really thought this whole death threat business would be a solid lead. But if this is the only one, I think we've hit a dead end."

Nino folded the paper neatly into a little square and put it in his pocket. Then he said, "Mr. Puglisi, got a minute?"

Nino turned toward the kitchen, mumbled, "excuse us," and walked out of the room.

Peewee leaned close to me and dropped his voice to a whisper. "Don't mind Nino's curtness. He isn't what you'd call a people person."

Then he followed his assistant into the kitchen. While Peewee and I had been looking at the ominous note, Nat had been checking out Nino's desk.

I joined him there.

"What do you make of that note? A Bible verse? And Nino seemed sort of weird about the whole thing. In general, he seems weird."

"Bernie—"

"I know, that's judgmental, but listen, I feel there's a lot this guy isn't telling us. You should see his bedroom, it's—"

"Bernie, stop talking," Nat whispered, "and take a look."

He'd opened the book on Nino's desk, right where it had been bookmarked. It was the beginning of a chapter.

"Holy moly."

The chapter title was "How garroting works—a step-by-step explanation."

At that moment, Nino and Peewee returned, and Nat and I pretended to be interested in the nearest bookshelves. We lapsed into small talk. Nat asked Peewee more questions about his books and got such detailed answers that I thought I'd never enjoy reading a novel again.

But I was only half-listening. Because out of the corner of my eye, I was watching Nino. He'd spotted the book on his desk.

He tensed. Muttered something under his breath.

And quickly stuffed the book onto a nearby shelf.

**6**

———

After the Wednesday morning rush was over, I took the opportunity to step into Angelica's office at Moroni's and make a phone call. I let it ring, and ring, and ring. The voicemail recording kicked in: "*Hello, you've reached Roberta LaRosa. Leave a message.*"

"Roberta, it's Bernie. Again. Call me."

I hung up, having little hope of getting a call back. I'd called Roberta from work yesterday afternoon, tried again in the evening, and then early this morning before getting to Moroni's. I wanted to ask her about Nino. But she was ignoring me.

I sighed, pocketed my phone, and went back to my station at the cash register.

Nat had arrived while I was out back, and he was leaning against the counter, talking to Angelica.

"So Mrs. Viola's assigned me to another inventory project. I have to go through everything we have on local murder cases over the past 20 years. Books. Photographs. Newspaper articles. I figure I'll be done in time for my retirement."

"At least she's trusting you with a big project," Angelica said, as she served him a plate with *bomboloni*, Italian donuts filled with pastry cream. "That sounds like progress."

"You know what I love about you, Angelica? You really believe everyone's got goodness inside them."

"Well, most people do, don't they?"

Nat and I exchanged a smile. I put an arm around Angelica and pulled her to me in half a hug.

"You can convert the worst cynic to an optimist," I said.

"And if your sunny disposition fails," Nat said, his mouth so full of donut and cream that his words got muffled, "your *bomboloni* will do the trick."

I made myself a cappuccino. While I steamed the milk, I mentioned Nino's reaction to finding the book on his desk.

"Strange," I said.

"Strange," Nat agreed, "but maybe not out of character. The guy's as socially awkward as an ostrich. Plus, he's got a bad case of OCD. And anyway, the book itself isn't as incriminating as I'd thought."

Nat explained he'd gone back over Peewee's books last night.

"You know, garroting appears more often than I remembered. So there's a perfectly logical explanation for Nino reading that book. And maybe there's a reasonable explanation for Roberta's visit, too."

"There is," I said. "He's in witness protection."

Angelica's eyebrows shot up. "No ..."

"Yes. It's the only explanation. Look, if I'd noticed Roberta was spying on Nino at Milano Books, then I might've suspected he was involved in criminal activity, and it somehow concerned her. Maybe that she was working a case with the FBI or DEA. But she wasn't just keeping an eye on him. She was visiting him. Inside his home. And there's only one reason Roberta LaRosa makes house calls."

Nat nodded. "Makes sense. But you know what else makes sense? For Marco Puglisi, creator of the greatest fictional mafia hitman ever, to have an assistant who's a former mobster himself. Especially if that ex-mobster briefly worked at a prison library."

Angelica shook her head, clearly amazed by the revelation. "Our own Nino Clemenza, a member of the mafia ..."

Nat laughed. "Angelica, you seem so shocked. And yet you don't think twice about gabbing with Primo Leone over an espresso and a plate of pignoli cookies."

"That's different. That's Primo."

Nat shook his head, amused by her reaction.

But I saw Angelica's point. Primo was different. He was out in the open, and had been for a long time. His history with the mafia was, well, history. But if Nino was in witness protection, his past might still have one foot in the present.

"Do you think Peewee knows?" I asked Nat.

"He did act as if the USPS truck was just a USPS truck."

"True. But if he knew Nino was in witness protection, would he reveal it to us?"

"Maybe he knows, but Nino doesn't know he knows, or Peewee suspects but doesn't know exactly what and Nino's told him some of it, but not all of it, or ..."

"Enough." I rubbed my temples. "This mystery's giving me a headache."

Nat said his goodbyes and headed out—he had boxes and boxes of archival material waiting for him back at the historical society.

Angelica and I soon got busy with the lunch and post-lunch crowds, and I welcomed the distraction. The busier I was making coffee and serving cookies and cannolis, the less preoccupied I was with a cagey U.S. Marshall, missing garrote wires, and clingy thriller writers who saw themselves as the next Sherlock Holmes.

Toward the end of the afternoon, a middle-aged woman and her teenage daughter came into Moroni's to pick up a box of cannoli. The woman greeted Angelica in a manner that managed to be polite, insincere, and condescending all at once.

"We're fortunate to have your little bakery," she said, "when we don't have time to drive to another."

She seemed to have quite a talent for nuance. Even the way she swiped her credit card suggested she was loath to touch anything in the bakery, lest she dirty and demean herself.

"Charlene, always great to see you," Angelica said. "And it's nice to see you again, too, Vicky."

Charlene's daughter smiled. Those straight teeth and calculating eyes sent goosebumps down my arms.

All of a sudden, I was twelve years old and Jennifer Jensen, queen bee of middle school, was blocking access to my locker, gritting her teeth at me. Without knowing a thing about this Vicky, I immediately disliked her. I could smell it —she reeked of bully.

"Vicky Bello is one our contestants," Angelica explained to me.

"Oh," I said. "Great."

I pictured Vicky with a cream pie all over her face and it made me feel a little better. But my happiness was short-lived. Because at that moment, Lily pushed through the door.

She came to a dead stop when she saw the Bellos.

Angelica greeted Lily warmly, then addressed both girls. "Are you two ready for the competition briefing tomorrow? The judges will all be there to go over the rules."

Lily nodded without saying a word.

"I know the rules," Vicky said.

"It's a formal thing," Angelica said. "It doesn't hurt anyone to hear the rules again, and it's like a warm-up to the semi-finals on Friday afternoon."

"I'm warmed up." Vicky gave Lily a nasty smirk. "I might as well skip straight to the finals. But Lily, I can understand if you feel you need more time to prepare. This competition is a big deal and—"

Her next thinly veiled insult was cut short by her phone. She looked at the screen, then pressed the phone to her ear as she hurried to the back of the cafe for some privacy. She spoke in rapid whispers. But some teenagers are as good at whispering as bulls are at traipsing quietly through china shops. I caught most of what she said.

"Daddy, I'm in the middle of something ... yes, Mom told me to tell you that ... I know, but she said even though it's your weekend, I could stay with her ... all right, I'll tell her you said so ... yes, I will, Daddy."

She returned to the counter, and her mom was glaring at her. Charlene Bello grabbed her daughter by the arm, and said, "We have work to do, young lady."

As Vicky was hauled out of Moroni's, she said, "Hey, let go ... what's the matter with you?"

After they'd left, I handed Lily an almond-paste cookie. She looked like she needed some sugar. She took it, mumbled something about needing to go anyway because of homework, and abandoned the cookie on the counter. She trudged out, head down, hands in her pockets. Her excitement at coming to Moroni's had clearly evaporated.

"Oh, I hope Lily crushes that brat," I told Angelica.

"I don't like Vicky's attitude, either. But her parents divorced a few years ago, and it got ugly. The girl's caught in the middle."

"As usual, you're making me feel sympathy for someone I don't want to feel sympathy for."

Even though we were alone, Angelica dropped her voice to a whisper. "I still want Lily to win."

"Angelica!" I said, shocked at her out-of-character confession. "Can you even say that as a judge?"

"The judges taste the cakes without knowing who baked them. So the best cake will win." Angelica looked out the window, craning her neck, apparently trying to catch a last glimpse of Lily. "Even if the best person doesn't."

I was sweeping the floor, getting ready to close Moroni's, when the door opened and the little bell jingled. Sofia Ruggiero and Rose Calabrese fluttered inside, talking a million miles a minute, half in English, half in Italian dialect. Bringing up the rear was Father Bruno, his unassuming, doe-like expression carrying a hint of amusement as he watched his companions crowd the display counter and argue about which cannolis to order.

"Nice to see you again, Bernie," Father Bruno said. "We've come to buy enough cannolis to placate at least a dozen septuagenarians."

"Are you having a party?"

"It's Wednesday poker night at St. Joseph's."

I couldn't hide my surprise. "Poker night? At the church?"

Father Bruno laughed. As soft and gentle as the burbling of a brook. "It might seem unorthodox. Yet the Catechism states that games of chance aren't bad, per se—they are morally unacceptable when a person becomes enslaved to the passion for gambling."

"Like Rose is," Sofia quipped.

"I am not enslaved to the passion for gambling." Rose got a mischievous look on her face. "But Sofia might be enslaved to the passion for a certain widower who'll be at poker night."

Sofia threw her hands into air. "*Maronna mia,* don't anybody respect privacy anymore?"

"In fact," Father Bruno continued, ignoring Sofia and Rose's antics, "there was a parish priest in South Carolina whose poker talents were so prodigious that he went on a TV poker show and beat three opponents, including a professional poker champion. In the final round, he held his rosary and prayed. He won $100,000, all funding for his parish. And he did the whole thing with the blessing of his bishop—and dare I say, God himself."

"Oh, you should do that, Father," Sofia said.

"Yes." Rose clapped her hands together. "I can see the headlines now: *Father Bruno, poker champion, wins grand prize.*"

Father Bruno chuckled softly. "Only divine intervention could keep me from losing all my pennies to you two tonight. I don't predict an illustrious career as a poker champion—on or off television."

They selected an assortment of cannolis. Then Father Bruno asked for a box of *pizzelles.* "My favorite," he said. "It reminds me of the Eucharist. In fact, *pizzelles* go well with red wine."

I was constantly amazed at how my assumptions about people could be challenged—Father Bruno wasn't what I'd believed him to be.

He thanked me for the cookies.

"We're all very excited about the Junior Baking Competition," he said. "And to see who will be crowned the champion."

Which made me think of Lily again. And then I realized what day it was.

"Oh, no," I said, looking at the clock on the wall. "Lily."

~

Hurrying home from Moroni's, I found Lily waiting on my doorstep, a big backpack over her shoulders. I'd almost forgotten about our agreement to meet, and I was relieved that Father Bruno's comment had reminded me. The last thing I wanted to do was let Lily down the week of her competition.

Lily held up a thermal bag and smiled. "I brought samples."

"Ooh, I can't wait to taste them. Come on in."

My ranch-style house might not impress the likes of Peewee Puglisi, but the size was perfect for me. I loved its coziness. Paintings by local artists graced the walls. I'd also bought some pretty statuettes and clay figurines at Mamma Mia's, the charity store in town.

"You have a beautiful home," Lily said, admiring my little kitchen-and-living-room combo.

"I don't use the kitchen as much as I should. I hope I've got what you need."

Lily took off her backpack and patted it. "I've got all my tools with me."

She got started, and as she worked on her cake, I sat at the kitchen island on a stool, drinking seltzer and talking to her. Or rather, listening to her. I'd never heard Lily chatter so much. It made me happy to hear how excited she was about the competition.

"I'm doing a chocolate torte for the competition. My own recipe. It's what got me to the semi-finals. Here, try this. It isn't perfect, but I'm getting close."

She opened the thermal bag and brought out a Tupperware with slices of chocolate torte. She got a napkin and carefully lifted a slice and handed it to me.

I bit into the torte. It was rich and earthy and tangy, and so smooth it was like biting into butter.

I groaned with pleasure. "Oh, come on. You're killing me, Lily."

She laughed. "It's good?"

"It's delicious."

She had other samples in the bag. A strawberry-cheese-cake torte. A chocolate eclair. And finally a Tupperware full of cannoli.

"Holy moly, Lily, you've been busy."

"Try the cannoli and tell me what you think." Lily frowned. "And be honest."

I bit into the pistachio cannoli. The cone crunched between my teeth, giving way to the sweet richness of the ricotta cream. I closed my eyes, savoring the taste.

"Perfect," I said.

"You really think so? I must've made hundreds, no, thousands of cannolis to try to get close to Angelica's."

"These definitely remind me of Angelica's."

Lily beamed. She continued working on her chocolate torte, combining her eggs, sugar, vanilla, and salt in my mixer, and then using a spatula to fold the mixture into the chocolate-butter-amaretto mass in a separate bowl. Once it was all mixed, she spooned the batter into a springform pan.

Then placed it in the oven in a roasting pan, which she filled with boiling water.

"Now it has to bake for about 40 minutes," she explained.

I was impressed by how professional she seemed. She worked the way Angelica worked, with a meticulous attention to detail, precision, and patience.

*You could never do that.*

I sighed. The little voice in my head was right. I would've tried to skip a step or two, which was no doubt why my cakes tended to collapse. Unless I had Angelica supervising me.

*Oh, Angelica, with someone like Lily, Moroni's would flourish even more …*

I'd been trained as an actress. I could scrape by as a barista. But I was no baker.

Nor did I love baking the way that Lily did—her passion for every detail was apparent in the way she focused deeply on even the smallest sprinkle of salt or sugar.

Watching her, I envied her, and that little voice in my head whispered that maybe I ought to have gone back to what I was good at: Eve Silver. After all, nothing was stopping me from contacting my old agent in California and exploring the possibility of acting again. Maybe there was even a chance that someone wanted to produce an Eve Silver TV show.

Then I remembered Father Bruno's story of the parishioner who'd left the mafia. He'd struggled to find the right path. He'd envied those who'd stayed on the path, and he'd envied those who'd found a vastly different one.

Father Bruno's story didn't have an ending. He hadn't revealed the man's destination. But the point was that the guy hadn't turned around and gone back. Much of my own journey, I was beginning to realize, still lay ahead. Witness protection had transformed me from Bernadette into Bernie. But the transformation wasn't complete.

Maybe that was why I kept allowing myself to be distracted by murder mysteries. Maybe I was kidding myself when I said that I didn't want to help Chief Tedesco with the investigation—I'd always known that I wouldn't transform into an extraordinary baker, the kind Angelica deserved by her side.

The investigation wasn't just a distraction. It was my chrysalis, my process of transformation, my—

*Enough already. Forget about the investigation. Right now you're helping Lily.*

I shoved aside my thoughts of my own journey and focused on Lily's instead.

We sat at the kitchen island, drinking seltzers, and talking.

"One moment I'm excited and confident," she was telling me. "I can see how this competition can be the beginning of something amazing. Like I'll look back years from now and say, *That's when it all started.*" She frowned. "But then I get worried and start to doubt myself. What if I lose? I'll definitely lose. And what will happen then? Will this be the moment I look back on and think, *Well, that's how my dreams of becoming a baker ended.*"

"It's one competition, Lily. If you don't win this one, there'll be others."

"Bernie, I don't live in New York City. Carmine is far from everything. If I can't impress the local judges here, what chance do I have of winning anything anywhere else?"

She hugged herself.

"I feel like I'm on this highway and there's an exit up

ahead and I've only got this one chance to get off and if I miss it ..."

"Sounds like I-95," I said.

But then I grew serious. Lily had her own troubles with finding the right path. Most people did. It was why you needed friends to stand by your side.

"Lily, listen, your doubt is just a sign that you're nervous. That's natural. And it's healthy."

"I sure am nervous." She leaned toward me, conspiratorially. "Yesterday, I was so nervous, I ate a whole bowl of cookie batter. I couldn't help myself."

She laughed, and it was like a ray of sunshine dispelling darkness—bright and cheerful. I laughed with her. We swapped stories of indulging in comfort food, from cookie batter to pizza for breakfast. Soon, the last signs of Lily's anxiety had vanished, and we were laughing until we had to wipe tears from our eyes.

The more time I spent with Lily, the more I liked her. And the more I liked her, the more I wanted her to win the Junior Baking Competition.

If only there was more I could do to help.

## 7

I bit into Lily's chocolate torte. It was amazingly soft, like butter. The deep, rich flavor filled my mouth, and from there, it seemed to glide straight down my throat and into my heart.

"Honestly?"

"Honestly," Lily said.

"This has got to be a winner."

I was gushing about its perfection, and Lily was laughing at the many adjectives I used—*perfect, bold, exceptional, awe-inspiring*—when my phone rang. My lock screen said the call was from Chief Tedesco.

"Bernie, you busy? Got plans tonight? No? Good. Because I'm treating you to dinner at Carlo's."

"You're buying me dinner? Are you feeling all right, chief?"

"*Maronna mia,*" she exclaimed. "Don't make this harder than it is. Just be there at 7 pm sharp."

I told her I'd be there. Honestly, I didn't need convincing to eat dinner at Carlo's, which was hands down Carmine's best restaurant.

Lily and I cleaned up my kitchen. She put the rest of her torte in a Tupperware, packing it into the thermal bag. With her backpack on her back, she waved goodbye, and I watched her walk down Lampedusa Lane with a happy spring to her step.

My heart squeezed tight. Oh, how I wanted Lily to win that competition.

I let the thought go and instead focused on what Chief Tedesco might want. I got on my canary yellow bicycle—my only vehicle—and pedaled to Garibaldi Avenue. I parked in the alley behind Carlo's Restaurant.

Carlo Moroni himself greeted me as I came through the front door. His pot belly looked a little rounder, his black goatee more closely trimmed, but otherwise, Angelica's brother was the same as always: warm and welcoming.

"Bernie, I'm so glad to see you—come in, come in."

As usual, entering Carlo's Restaurant was a sure-fire way of lowering my blood pressure. The thickly carpeted floor softened my step—I was tempted to remove my shoes and walk barefoot—while the heavy velvet drapes framing the front windows muted all sounds. Low music played from hidden speakers. Tonight it was a mellow selection of Italian arias. Puccini. Verdi. Bellini. Along with selections from Mozart's Italian operas.

Since moving to Carmine, I'd become quite familiar with not only Italian crooners but also the greatest hits of opera.

Carlo led me to a table for two against the wall, where Chief Tedesco was already seated, drinking a glass of water and studying the menu as if it were a forensics report.

"Maria will be right with you," Carlo said, and eyed Tedesco with a frown. Ever since Maria had been the prime suspect in a murder, Carlo had held a grudge against the chief of police.

I sat down. Maria Ferrante, the restaurant's only waitress, and Anthony Ferrante's sister, delivered steaming plates of sausage and peppers to a nearby table before turning her attention to ours.

She gave me a big smile. "Great to see you, Bernie. You too, chief. Let me tell you about the specials. Tonight, we're serving a special seafood dish from the Adriatic Coast in Italy called *baccalà arracanato*. Salt cod baked with breadcrumbs, lots of oregano, tomatoes, raisins, olives, and pine nuts, plus fennel seeds."

"Sounds delicious," I said.

"Then there's the chicken scarpariello. Slow-braised chicken thighs in a vinegar sauce with sweet Italian sausage, onions, and peppers."

"Can't go wrong with chicken," Chief Tedesco said. "Or sausage and peppers."

"But let's not forget the meatballs," Maria added. "My own favorite: *Polpette alla Napoletana*. Neapolitan meatballs."

I groaned. "You can't keep throwing more and more delicious options at us."

"Actually, we have two meatball recipes," Carlo said, butting in on our conversation with Maria. "*Polpette alla Napoletana,* and my classic *prupetti*—Sicilian meatballs."

Maria frowned. "I recommend the *polpette*. They're something else."

"The *prupetti* are more flavorful," Carlo said.

"The *polpette* are classic."

"And what are my *prupetti* if not classic?"

Carlo turned to me. Maria to Chief Tedesco.

"You gotta try the *prupetti*," Carlo said.

"The *polpette*," Maria insisted.

I laughed. "You two always have to fight about every-thing, don't you? Listen, there's an easy solution. We'll order both kinds of meatballs, and the chief and I will share."

Carlo clapped a hand to his belly. "Brilliant!"

Maria smiled. "A good solution."

"Now," Carlo said, "about the wine ..."

Once we'd found a compromise on the wine and Carlo and Maria had hurried off, I leaned forward, looking Chief Tedesco in the eye.

"Well? What's this all about? Inviting me to dinner at Carlo's is about as incriminating as a confession. Only I don't know what crime you've committed."

Chief Tedesco rearranged her knife and fork, avoiding my eyes. "Marco Puglisi."

"Peewee?"

"I needed to get rid of him. So I dumped him on your lap."

"I knew it!"

Once I'd enjoyed watching her squirm a little more, I asked the obvious question.

"But why? I mean, I understand he's ..."

"A pain in the *culo*. Bernie, he's more than that. He's a liability. Remember he said he'd worked with the FBI? It's not entirely true. He has a friend in the FBI, who's also a real pain in the *culo*. Lives nearby. Feels he's got a responsibility to the community, so he loves to butt in on my jurisdiction."

"Ah, I see. Peewee wants to shoehorn himself into your investigation, and so he uses his friend as leverage."

"Bingo."

I smiled. "Don't worry. I'm happy to help. And even happier to be treated to dinner at Carlo's. Besides, snooping around with Peewee has yielded some interesting information."

I filled her in on my latest discoveries, saving the biggest detail for last—that Nino Clemenza was in witness protection.

"I already know," Chief Tedesco said.

"You do?" Then I smacked my forehead. "Of course you do."

Often the U.S. Marshalls Service would work with local law enforcement to keep a person safe. Chief Tedesco had known about my true identity when I was first placed in witness protection in Carmine. So I should've guessed the same would apply to Nino.

Our food arrived on two platters with serving spoons, so we could dish up and share. The two kinds of meatballs were served with sides of pasta and broccoli rabe. Chief Tedesco and I dug into the meal.

The Neapolitan meatballs were light and airy, lightened with milk-soaked breadcrumbs, and sharpened with a salty Pecorino cheese. In contrast, the Sicilian meatballs were sweet—raisins and pine nuts made them at once sweet, juicy, and crunchy—yet the addition of provolone and Parmesan cheeses deepened the savory flavor. We washed down the delicious food with Carlo's best Chianti.

It was difficult to think of murder when our tastebuds were so preoccupied by meatballs, but we did our best.

"Do you think Peewee knows?" I asked. "I mean, they've worked closely together for years. Peewee writes crime thrillers. You'd think he might've guessed."

"True. But sometimes when the obvious is right in front of you, you dismiss it as too obvious. Peewee's author mind might suspect everyone of being a criminal, and so his rational conclusion is that nobody actually is."

"So what is Nino's background?"

"Oh, you know I can't talk about that. But rest assured,

we've considered Nino—and ruled him out. All that's behind him. He wouldn't be in Carmine if he didn't want a new life. Plus, you know the stats on recidivism among convicted criminals in witness protection."

I knew the stats. People who started new lives under new names tended to truly turn over a new leaf. In a way, I could relate. Even though I hadn't committed any crimes, witness protection had inspired me to embrace my assumed identity.

I leaned across the table and lowered my voice. "What about Peewee?"

"Peewee Puglisi?" Chief Tedesco shook her head. "He was the first person I looked into, and he's simply got no motive. He'd had some trouble with Anne and he was planning to let her go. If anything, Anne had a reason to kill him. Not the other way around."

For some reason, my mind flashed on Roberto Rizzoli. But I pushed the idea aside. Chief Tedesco must've considered Roberto already—and the guy was supposed to be a saint.

"So if Nino and Peewee aren't suspects," I asked, "who is?"

"At the book event, there was a thriller writer. He'd once been represented by Anne Adams. But after his publisher dropped him, she did too. He's now back to his old day job. Which he hates. He blames Anne. Then he turns up at Milano Books on Saturday and sticks around for the after party. He was seen coming out of the back office, supposedly because he mistook the door for the restroom."

"And the murder weapon?"

"We hope to find it when we search his home in Livingston. Along with the missing briefcase. We're working closely with the Livingston Police Department and waiting for a judge to approve a warrant. Any minute now, I might get a call."

"Then the case might be solved soon."

"I'm counting on it."

After the heavy meal, I welcomed the bike ride home. I found my canary yellow bicycle in the alley and rolled it out to Garibaldi Avenue.

I looked up and down the street.

Carmine was peaceful in the dimness of evening. The street lamps cast a warm glow, but the shadows were deep and dark now that we were marching through fall, heading toward winter. We were still in that wonderful stage of the season, where the air was fresh and cool without being cold, ideal for spending time outside enjoying the reds and yellows of the fall foliage.

A poster on a lamp post advertised an upcoming Halloween event in Puccini Park.

A police cruiser drove down Garibaldi and Officer Fontana waved at me. I waved back. Otherwise there wasn't much traffic. Further down the street, a car idled by the curb.

I swung onto my bike and pushed off from the curb.

I pedaled slowly, enjoying the fresh air and the scenery. I passed Moroni's. Then, further up Garibaldi, I turned onto Da Vinci Street.

A woman was out walking her poodle. Two men sat on a porch under a light—it looked like a young man and his grandfather—drinking beer. Further along, I spotted a couple standing on their stoop, kissing each other.

It was difficult to imagine now, but when I'd first come to

Carmine, I'd wanted to leave at once. I'd begged Roberta LaRosa to transfer me to a big city where I could blend in. But Roberta had given me two options: Carmine or a remote cabin in northern Alaska. Even thinking about the cabin made me shudder. Winter in New Jersey was cold enough for me, thank you very much.

How could I ever have considered leaving Carmine? I couldn't imagine it now. The town felt more like home than any other place I'd ever lived in. The people had become family.

Reflecting on my journey to Carmine reminded me of what Father Bruno had told me about there being different paths. More than just two. The problem was that whenever I entertained the thought of changing the path I traveled on, it felt like a rejection of what I'd embraced: Carmine, Moroni's, Angelica.

But I knew what Father Bruno would say. He'd say those three things weren't the same. That I could live in Carmine and be friends with Angelica without devoting my career to Moroni's.

Goosebumps prickled my skin.

I didn't want to think about it. I didn't want to think about anything but the fall leaves overhead, the warm glow from within the houses on Da Vinci Street, and the car trailing behind me ...

*Hold on ...*

I glanced over my shoulder again.

There it was. A car drifting up Da Vinci, its headlights turned off, apparently in an attempt to remain undetected. If the damn thing had kept its lights on, I might not have worried. But a car with tinted windows that followed me without its headlights on—that was textbook trouble.

I pedaled faster.

The car's engine revved.

I pushed down on the pedals with all my weight, rising off my seat to put more strength into it, and go faster.

The headlights came on. If they had been floodlights, they couldn't have been more blinding. I pumped the pedals and swerved recklessly onto Lampedusa Lane.

I flew into my driveway, almost crashing into my house. I dropped my bicycle on the lawn and sprinted to the door.

My keys got caught on a thread inside my jeans and I tugged and tugged—and finally ripped them free. Then struggled to get the house key into the lock.

I turned the lock, then shouldered the door open, throwing myself into the hallway. I slammed the door. I locked it—and pushed the bolt into place.

After listening for a moment, I hurried into the living room, where, panting, I peeked through the curtains.

My heart hammered in my chest.

My yellow bike lay on the lawn where I'd abandoned it. I gazed up the street. Then the other way.

No car.

In fact, nothing at all.

What color had it been? Something dark. I couldn't tell. I wasn't even sure what kind of car it had been.

I continued to watch the street for a long, long time, and by the time the dog walker with her poodle sauntered past, my heart was beginning to calm down.

No killer had tried to run me off the road. Or chase me into my house. So what had actually happened?

I slid down onto my couch and let out a long breath.

Nothing had really happened, had it? Had I even been threatened by that car—or had it been a random driver who, starting down the street, had realized they'd forgotten to turn on their headlights?

Yes, that must've been what happened.

*And then you freaked out, Bernie.*

I rubbed my hands across my face.

*This murder case is making you paranoid.*

Still, before I went to bed, I double checked my front door. It was locked and bolted. Good.

**8**

———

Next to the counter in Moroni's stood a board on an easel with the three semi-finalists' names: Victoria Bello, Enrico Marchetti, and Lily Salerno. It was the next day—Thursday—and the contestants sat at a table together, ready for the afternoon briefing on the competition rules. Friends and family sat at other tables or stood at the back—Charlene Bello, Mrs. Greco, Phil Palladino, and Peter Piatek, already snapping photos for the *Carmine Enquirer*—while the three judges stood by the easel: Angelica, Mrs. Viola, and Jerry from the Old Mill.

Mrs. Viola seemed an obvious choice. Even if she wasn't a connoisseur of baked goods, she had the stereotypical sternness of a competition judge. But Jerry's involvement surprised me.

When I asked him how he became a judge for Carmine's Junior Baking Competition, he shrugged.

"I like cake."

Angelica stepped forward and welcomed everyone. She'd placed complimentary pitchers of ice tea and platters of cookies on each table to ensure everyone had a treat.

After gushing about the contestants and their supportive friends and family, she introduced Mrs. Viola, who would explain the rules.

"The semi-finalists made it this far because they submitted original recipes that we judges chose as the most promising. Now the proof will be in the pudding." She eyed the three young people with stern skepticism. "There are rules you must observe. You will prepare your cakes at home in your own kitchens, but you must work alone. Frankly, if it were up to me, you'd bake your cakes under close supervision."

Angelica cleared her throat. "We operate on the honor system—you are all talented bakers, and we trust that you're part of this competition because you care about integrity, quality ingredients, and creating joy through baking."

Mrs. Viola muttered something under her breath about the integrity of youth. I didn't need to hear what she'd said to know it was negative. Then she said, "You must all deliver your semi-finalist cakes tomorrow, Friday, at the same time, at the same place—4 pm sharp here at Moroni's Italian Bakery. Any questions?"

Someone asked about how contestants continued to the finals.

"Sudden death," Mrs. Viola said. "Whoever's ranked third tomorrow drops out. Only two participants will compete in the finals on Saturday."

"And then only one will win," Vicky Bello said and smirked.

Lily frowned. Enrico Marchetti, whose broad shoulders made him a rowing coach's dream, leaned close to Lily and said, as if in confidence, but loud enough for everyone to hear, "Ignore her. Cakes are about sweetness, not bitterness."

I instantly liked the kid. And clearly, so did Lily, who smiled back at him. Vicky's face turned sour, and she made a show of turning her chair away from her two competitors and crossing her arms on her chest.

*Childish,* I thought. Then remembered what Angelica had said, and couldn't resist feeling sympathy for a kid whose parents had filled her with such bitterness.

It didn't change my desire to see Lily take first prize. Nor did it change my feelings about who should come in second: Enrico.

Mrs. Viola answered a few more questions from the audience, including why there wasn't a big cash prize.

Angelica stepped in. "The competition is—and always has been—about celebrating Carmine's young baking talents. The attention they get may help them if they want to pursue careers as bakers or patisserie chefs. But it's never been about money."

She continued to mention some of the junior talents who'd gone on to become successful, when my phone pinged. I dug it out of my apron and saw a message from Chief Tedesco.

> Bad news, Bernie. We searched the Livingston suspect's home and found nothing. No murder weapon. And no briefcase. So keep your eyes and ears open for me.

I could almost hear the disappointment in her voice. My own heart sank. I'd hoped she was right. I'd hoped the case was close to being solved. And yet ...

*You never believed she was right, did you?*

No, her theory that it was this thriller writer from Livingston hadn't convinced me. There were too many open questions around the people who had attended the book event on Saturday, people who were still right here in Carmine.

My mind was churning up the details of the case again, and as I tried to make sense of the welter of clues, people began to leave Moroni's.

One of the people who'd been listening to Angelica and Mrs. Viola speak came forward. It was Mrs. Greco.

"I'd like to order a delivery. A box of assorted cannoli. They're for my old friend, Nancy Rizzoli."

"Roberto's mother?"

"That's right. Roberto and his wife helped Nancy move to Lakeview yesterday, and I'd like to send them all a treat. My bridge club is meeting in 20 minutes. Otherwise, I would deliver it myself."

"What a nice idea."

I grabbed a cake box and began filling it with cannoli. Then, remembering Chief Tedesco's request that I keep my eyes and ears open, I had an idea.

"In fact, Mrs. Greco, I'll deliver them myself."

Lakeview Assisted Care Facility was located a few blocks off Da Vinci Street, not far from my own home. The long, two-story building had been done in the Arts and Crafts Style of architecture—cabin-like wood beams, a long porch under a low roof, eye-catching gables, with curved woodwork that evoked something from Grimm's fairy tales. A brownstone chapel stood next to the main building. Between the two structures, a path led to a garden in the back, and I glimpsed a greenhouse and a small pond.

Was this supposed to be the lake the facility's name referred to? In any case, Carmine Lake was nowhere near—even if you climbed the gable, you wouldn't be able to spy it in the distance. The name "Lakeview" was probably more about evoking a feeling than actually promising a clear view of a large body of water.

I would ask Nancy Rizzoli about that. Then I'd ask her a few questions about her son and her daughter-in-law—the present and the previous one. Maybe she'd reveal a thing or two.

Or maybe I was on a wild goose chase.

I sauntered into the reception, box of cannolis in my hands, acting as casually and confidently as I could. In an episode of *Silver & Gold*, Eve Silver had snuck into a private clinic to visit an important witness to a crime by pretending to deliver a box of chocolates. The dialogue that the *Silver & Gold* writing team had crafted might come in handy.

I gave the guy in the reception a big smile.

"Delivery from Moroni's for Mrs. Rizzoli."

"You can leave it right here. I'll make sure she gets it."

"I've got a personal message to go with it."

"Nice touch," the guy said and grabbed a pen and paper. "What is it?"

"Personal. As in, I'd better deliver it personally. It's our policy at Moroni's to deliver in person."

"We have a policy, too." He gave me an understanding smile. "It's probably more legally binding than the one from Moroni's."

If the writers on *Silver & Gold* had written more dialogue, I couldn't remember it. Besides, Eve had more or less been allowed to waltz right into the clinic. Now I saw how unrealistic that had been.

I made up a message from Mrs. Greco to go with the

card, which already probably contained a much more personal one than the one I'd concocted. And then I handed over the box.

Stepping outside, I considered—and not for the first time—how much easier detective work was on TV. I was grumbling to myself about my bad luck, when I glanced toward the garden. I stopped.

Two people were strolling across the grass, heading down to the pond.

It was Roberto and Gina Rizzoli.

They were talking, walking close to each other, giving their body language an air of confidentiality—of wandering off to share secrets. I couldn't know that for sure. But I did know that Lakeview would never allow me inside. This was my chance to get more information. As Chief Tedesco had said, *Keep your eyes and ears open.*

Before Roberto and Gina could turn around and see me, I hurried past the opening between the two buildings and hid behind the chapel. A path ran along the side of the chapel, and that brought me to a tall hedge ringing the property. I squeezed through a gap between the brownstone wall and the hedge and emerged among a cluster of apple trees.

From my hiding place among the trees, I had a good view of the pond, the greenhouse, and beyond that, the back of Lakeview's main building. Nearby, more apple trees spread out on the lawn as it sloped down to the pond.

Roberto and Gina continued to saunter in a wide arc around the pond. As they turned, their backs were to me, and I could safely move out of the copse of trees and dash over to an apple tree standing on its own. Then, from there, grateful for the soft grass and how it silenced my steps, I flew to the next tree.

As I got closer to the couple, I heard Gina raise her voice. She sounded upset. I crept closer, hiding behind a tree that put me only a stone's throw from the couple—assuming you had a weak arm and the stone was big.

Roberto said, "But we already talked this through, my angel. Mom just moved. We need to give her a couple of days to settle in."

"The longer we stay, the bigger the risk that—"

"I know, I know." He stopped, and so did she. He took her hands. "Look, I understand why you're so worried. But nobody will find out. OK? And if it makes you feel any better, we'll stay away from public places. We'll go from Lakeview to the hotel and back again. Nowhere else."

"Rob, I know how important your mom is to you. And to me, too. It's just—"

"This whole situation is stressful."

"It's terrible ..."

"I know, Gina."

They leaned close, touching heads. Gina whispered something I couldn't hear.

"Me too," Roberto said, taking a step back from her. "And soon we'll be home in Seattle, and everyone will forget about us. Meanwhile, we'll keep out of sight. While I'm visiting Mom, why don't you get out of Carmine? Away from people. Go for a hike by the lake. It's pretty up by the Overlook."

"I hiked around the Overlook yesterday, remember? That's when I stumbled on that cabin and that man. Nino Clemenza. It freaked me out. He freaked me out. Something about him is ... *off*." She grabbed his arm. "Roberto, do you think he knows?"

"How could he, Gina? Listen, forget about the Overlook, then. Hike the other side of the lake."

"Or I guess I could walk the Old Quarry Trail. I used to love how quiet it was up there."

"Honey, the Old Quarry Trail isn't there any more. Heavy rains made the path collapse into the quarry. It was closed a decade ago."

"Oh."

The sound of a phone ringing made them both look down. Roberto dug out his phone and looked at the screen. He frowned. "What now?"

As he answered his call, he and Gina turned. I pressed myself up against the tree, hoping they wouldn't see me. They passed within a few feet of me and I heard Roberto say, "How bad?"

He grunted.

"Not good."

Then they were past me and heading up the lawn, past the pond. They were approaching the Lakeview's back porch. I could no longer hear what they were saying.

But I'd already heard a lot. Most of it was difficult to make sense of. But one thing stood out to me: If Gina had never visited Carmine before, as she'd told me, then how could she know about an old trail by the quarry?

**9**

———

After leaving Lakeview, I called Angelica. It was nearing the end of the workday, and she said she'd take care of things and lock up—I could go home early.

Instead, I headed for the public library.

At the circulation desk, I found Nat helping Father Bruno check out a stack of books.

When I saw which books the Catholic priest was checking out, I was surprised.

*Strong Poison.*

*The ABC Murders.*

*The Poisoned Chocolates Case.*

"Father Bruno," I said. "These are not the kinds of books I thought you'd read."

"Oh, I read all kinds of books."

"But books about murders ..."

He raised an eyebrow. "Have you read the Bible, Bernie? Parts of it are not exactly PG-13. I think I can handle a little homicide."

He made a good point. I always thought of the life-affirming statements and moral lessons by Jesus, but some of the stories in the Old Testament, in particular, were brutal.

"Besides, I listen to people's problems day in and day out," Father Bruno said. "Their concerns, anxieties, confessions. Then I try to bring comfort. And I'd be sinning if I lied and told you it wasn't exhausting."

"All done," Nat said.

Father Bruno thanked him and picked up his stack of murder mysteries. "You see, Bernie, sometimes at the end of a tough day, it's just nice to know that someone's gonna get whacked."

After Father Bruno left, Nat and I exchanged a smile.

"I don't disagree with him," Nat said. "Anyway, what brings you to the library? If you want to borrow any Golden Age mysteries, I'm sorry to disappoint you—Father Bruno's cleaned us out."

"I went to Lakeview."

"You're getting old," Nat said with a wink, "but not *that* old."

I swatted him—or tried to. He ducked away, laughing.

"Seriously," I said. "I overheard Gina and Roberto talking."

Then I recounted what I'd heard in the garden, and Nat grew serious.

"This calls for a drink at the Old Mill. Hold on. I'll tell Mrs. Viola goodbye. Her office is in the back."

I followed Nat down a corridor, past the historical society's exhibition room. He stopped at a door with a brass plaque that said, "Head Curator."

He knocked. "Mrs. Viola?"

No answer.

"Maybe she had an appointment elsewhere," Nat said.

I had a terrible sense of déjà vu. In *Silver & Gold*, people were always knocking on doors and getting no answer right before discovering a body.

Nat turned to go.

"You're not going to open the door?" I asked, incredulous.

"Why would I? It's Mrs. Viola's office. I've never set foot inside. I doubt she'd appreciate me snooping—oh, wait. I see. You do want to snoop."

"I don't. I just want to check on her. Make sure she's OK."

"She's fine, Bernie. You're getting paranoid."

He grabbed the door handle, turned it, and pushed the door open.

"See?" he said, extending a hand to show me the office within. "Nothing unusual."

Except he was wrong. There was something unusual within.

"Nat, take a look at this."

I stepped inside.

It was a small office with a single desk as well as a small sofa-and-armchair set arranged around a low table, no doubt for when Mrs. Viola hosted meetings. The desk was tidy. It held a computer and a cactus and a framed photograph of a young couple that, judging by the dated clothes they wore, might be Mrs. Viola's parents.

But the interesting thing was not the drab decor. It was the cork board behind the desk.

Pinned to the board were dozens of photographs, printouts, and even a map of Carmine marked with dots and lines. The whole thing looked like a police department's major incident room.

At the center of the web of photos and other items was a recognizable face.

"Anne Adams," Nat said.

A nearby photo of Gina had been circled with a thick, red marker.

"Looks like Mrs. Viola is running an investigation of her own," I said.

Nat nodded. "And she suspects Gina of killing Anne."

That sent a chill down my spine.

"Nat," I said. "I could use that drink now."

"**I**s everyone in this town an amateur detective?" I complained as Nat and I entered the Old Mill. "Between you, Mrs. Viola, and Peewee Puglisi, it sure is getting crowded."

I was looking forward to talking to Nat at the Old Mill, but we'd just reached the bar when someone called out our names.

Peewee and Nino were sitting in a booth, and Peewee was waving at us, a big, goofy smile on his face. I couldn't think of an excuse for not joining them. Apparently, Nat couldn't either.

With a sigh, I headed toward them and Nat followed.

Minutes later, Peewee, Nat, Nino, and I were each nursing a red ale. They were the happy hour special. Jerry had a thing for drinks specials that were red—of course, in tribute to Carmine, the crimson pigment that gave our town its name.

I was telling them all about what I'd heard Roberto and Gina say, leaving out the part about bumping into Nino in the woods. In fact, I felt uneasy talking about the case in front of Nino, who simply sat in silence, hardly touching his beer.

"Would you say they were acting guilty?" Peewee asked me.

"Guilty, suspicious, or plain secretive. Maybe all three."

I'd given my impressions of Roberto and Gina a lot of thought. One minute, I was convinced they'd basically confessed to the murder. The next, I wasn't so sure. And I couldn't forget the thick red marker Mrs. Viola had used to circle Gina's face in that photo on the cork board.

"There's something we're missing," I said. "Some reason Gina wants to stay out of sight until they go home."

I told them about Gina's knowledge of the old trail by the quarry.

"That suggests Gina's visited Carmine before," Peewee said.

"That old trail was shut down 10 years ago," Nat said. "So she must've visited a long time ago—and even if she's come back since, she definitely didn't go hiking for a while."

I shook my head. "None of it makes sense. If she visited town before, why keep it a secret?"

Peewee sipped his beer and frowned. "Unless ..."

"What?"

"No, I'm probably wrong."

He stared at his beer, his frown deepening, as if he were trying to remember something. On the jukebox Al Martino was singing, "Can't Take My Eyes Off You." I guess it was appropriate, since I couldn't take my eyes off Peewee.

"Come on, Peewee," Nat said. "Out with it."

"Well, at the event at Milano Books, I overheard Anne say something to Gina, and it upset her. It sounded like—"

I cut in. "'He'll cheat again.' I heard it too."

Peewee gave me a surprised look. Then he shook his head. "See, I knew I was wrong."

"What are you talking about?"

"Well, I didn't hear 'He'll cheat again.' I heard 'You're Rita Glen.'"

Nat gasped. "Rita Glen? You're sure?"

"Am I 100 percent sure?" Peewee shrugged. "No, but why? Who is Rita Glen? The name seems familiar ..."

"Yeah," I said. "It does sound familiar."

Nat dug out his phone from his pocket and tapped away at the screen. He swiped. He tapped again. Then looked up, gazing with surprising intensity at me through his fair bangs, and then Peewee, and then me again.

He put his phone on the table and turned it so we could see.

"This," he said, "is Rita Glen."

He'd used the public library website to bring up an old newspaper article. I recognized it from the historical society's exhibition. The headline said, "Carmine teenager kills classmate; police suspect foul play."

My heart did a cartwheel.

I grabbed Nat's phone and pinched my fingers to zoom in on the photograph.

"My God," I said. "Look at Rita's face."

Peewee and I leaned over the table, staring at Nat's phone. Even Nino took an interest, craning his neck to see.

Twenty years had passed. Her face had lost its baby fat, slimming down to harder angles. Crow's feet had gathered at the edges of her eyes. And yet, if you knew who you were looking at, you could tell what teenaged Rita Glen would look like today.

She'd look exactly like Gina Rizzoli.

∽

Friday morning. Chief Tedesco and I sat in her cruiser across the street from the Villa Medici, a boutique hotel on the outskirts on town. It was built in the 19th century Italianate style, with arched Venetian windows and a loggia on the second story—an exterior gallery supported by columns and arches. The building's color was a striking raspberry pink.

"Wow," I said. "The name really suits the building."

"Weren't the Medicis all murderers?" Tedesco said.

"You're thinking of the Borgias, Italy's first crime family."

"Right you are. And it turns out the thriller writer from Livingston is no Borgia. The most suspicious things we found at his place were a DVD boxed set of *Murder, She Wrote* and 20 years worth of Horticulture magazine, all the issues arranged in chronological order." She sighed. "This lead on the Rizzolis will probably turn out to be another dead end, too, but Gina lied to us about her past. I want to ask her a few questions."

Eve Silver would've been cool as a cucumber. Ready to leap out and confront the suspect. But I couldn't stop my foot from tapping the floor and my stomach made strange gurgling sounds.

There was a knock at the window, and I jumped.

Tedesco rolled it down.

Officer Fontana greeted her and said, "We're ready to go in."

"And it looks like someone's ready to go out," Chief Tedesco said, pointing toward the hotel's entrance.

Roberto and Gina Rizzoli emerged from the hotel, pulling two small, black suitcases behind them. Both looked harried. Primo's taxi appeared down the street and, approaching the Villa Medici, pulled up to the curb.

"Let's go," Tedesco told Fontana.

Fontana jogged across the street, his belt full of police gear, including his gun, jiggling. Before I'd struggled out of my seatbelt and gotten out of the car, Tedesco had caught up with him.

"Mr. and Mrs. Rizzoli," she called out.

By the time I joined Tedesco and Fontana, Roberto was busy explaining that a business emergency required him to go back to Seattle urgently. Primo rolled down his window and complained to Roberto and Gina that traffic would be hell on 287.

"A plane can fly over that mess," he said. "But I drive a cab. What can I do?"

Roberto turned to Chief Tedesco. "We've got a plane to catch from Newark."

"And we've got a few questions before you go," Tedesco said. "Starting with why you lied about your past, Mrs. Rizzoli? We know who you are—or who you used to be, 20 years ago."

Gina's eyes widened. Then her shoulders slumped, and she said, her voice tight with suppressed emotion, "See, Roberto? This is exactly why I didn't want to come back. People would find out. They'd treat me as if a day hadn't passed since I was a teenager and then—"

"*Ma che cozzo fai?*" Tedesco barked. She had a tendency to use more Italian when she got upset. "We're conducting a murder investigation. I don't care if the whole town shows up with pitchforks. You don't lie to a police officer, *capisce?*"

"You don't understand—"

"Oh, *I* don't understand? I think *you* don't understand. I could throw the book at you for lying and obstructing justice."

Roberto stepped closer to her, holding up his hands in a

gesture of peace. "Please. We meant no harm. We wanted to help my mother, and then leave as quietly as we came. If it hadn't been for the tragedy at the bookstore ..."

"Which I'm sure everyone will blame me for now," Gina said, crossing her arms on her chest. If it was an attempt to look defiant, it failed, because her lower lip was trembling, and her eyes welled up with tears.

"We've got nothing to hide," Roberto said.

"All right." Tedesco pointed to their suitcases. "Then you don't mind opening your luggage for us to take a look."

"Go ahead. As I said, we've got nothing to hide."

Fontana stepped forward and laid Gina's suitcase flat on the ground. He unzipped it. On top was a copy of the Bible and a book with the title, *Forgiveness: How God's Love Helps Us Heal Ourselves and Others*.

Fontana put on latex gloves and got started searching the bag. Clearly he'd done this work before. He managed to look through Gina's clothes and toiletries swiftly and thoroughly, and without making a complete mess. I was impressed.

"Nothing, chief."

He zipped up her suitcase. Then turned his attention to Roberto's, laying it flat, opening it, and—

He never got to show off his searching skills.

Inside Roberto's suitcase, two interesting items lay on top of the folded clothes.

One was an artifact from the Carmine Historical Appreciation & Preservation Society: the garroting wire. Tedesco pulled on a pair of latex gloves and picked up the murder weapon.

"*Maronna mia*," Primo said, hanging out of the window of his cab. "That don't look so good."

"That's not mine," Roberto said. "I've never seen it before."

The other item was a folded piece of paper.

As Tedesco unfolded it, I came closer. The letterhead had Anne Adams's name and business address. The brief, typed message said,

Dear Roberto,

I know who Gina is. If you want to keep your dirty little secret, bring $20,000 in cash to Milano Books on Saturday night. I'll bring a briefcase.

Don't let me down.

Anne

"I wouldn't kill Anne," Roberto protested. "I wouldn't kill anyone."

Chief Tedesco pulled a plastic bag out of her pocket, slipped the paper inside, and sealed it. Then she turned to Fontana.

"Officer Fontana, please read Mr. Rizzoli his rights."

**10**

___

The shock of the morning's discovery didn't wear off easily. At Moroni's, I moved through my tasks in a daze, serving one customer a *caffe longo* when he'd asked for a *latte*, and boxing up a dozen *amaretti*, when in fact the order had been for *anginetti*. By the afternoon, I felt I'd said, "I'm sorry," more than I'd said, "Thank you and have a nice day."

Angelica was setting up for the Junior Baking Competition, arranging the tables and the easel with the placard.

"You're a million miles away," she said.

"Only a couple miles, actually."

"Down at the police station?"

I nodded. "Gina was acting suspiciously, but now that I know what I know … honestly, I don't blame her. If I were her, I would want to keep my secret, too. She killed a classmate when she was a kid. But why would that logically make her a killer now, 20 years later? And nothing that I can see would make Roberto a killer."

"Aren't crimes often committed by the person closest to the victim?"

"True. But Roberto and Anne hadn't talked for ages. And it was Roberto who wanted to reconcile. Plus, what kind of killer skips town with the murder weapon neatly placed at the top of his suitcase?"

"Well, at least Mrs. Viola should be pleased that the garrote wire has been found."

But when Mrs. Viola arrived, she was anything but pleased. In fact, she was sobbing into a handkerchief.

"My Rob," she blew her nose noisily into her handkerchief. Then narrowed her eyes. "They got the wrong person."

I tended to agree, so I took note of what she said.

"It wasn't Roberto. It was that murderess, Gina." She wiped her nose. "I heard that their suitcases were identical. The tags said, *Mr. and Mrs. Rizzoli.* I know what happened. Gina was packing the murder weapon, and she was in such a hurry that she didn't realize she'd shoved it into Roberto's suitcase instead of her own. Yes, that must've been what happened."

Angelica gave me a look that showed profound sympathy with a heavy dose of skepticism.

And yet ...

Mrs. Viola's theory was fundamentally flawed, but she had pointed out an important fact: Roberto and Gina's suitcases were indistinguishable from each other. When Officer Fontana had opened Gina's, the clothes within had proven the bag belonged to her. But if someone was in a hurry, they might easily mistake one bag for the other. Say, if that someone was in a hurry to plant evidence.

I excused myself for a moment. In Angelica's small back office, I closed the door and called Chief Tedesco. The phone went to voice mail. So I called the station and got hold of Anthony Ferrante.

I explained my theory.

"Tell me something I don't already know, Bernie," he said. "Roberto and Gina claim they left their suitcases in the hotel lobby while they went for breakfast, and anyone could've tampered with them during that time."

"So Roberto was framed."

"Possibly," he said. "Or he's terrible at covering up his crime."

"Did staff see anyone suspicious?"

"Right now, Chief Tedesco is still questioning both the Rizzolis. Fontana's taking statements from staff. We'll see what comes of it."

I thought for a moment. There would be forensic analysis of the murder weapon. Interviews. Lots of attention paid to the Rizzolis. But in spite of the garrote wire turning up, another object was still missing.

"Any sign of Anne's briefcase?"

"No," Anthony said, and his answer was so curt, it gave me a hint of the frustration the police department felt. The absence of the briefcase might mean nothing. Or it might be the missing link to solving the case.

I hung up, feeling reassured that the police were handling the matter. But the idea that Roberto had been framed certainly changed things. It meant the killer wasn't in Livingston or New York City or some place far away. It meant the killer was right here in Carmine.

I was mulling this over, when my eyes fell on a wooden box on Angelica's desk. It had a little metal clasp. On the top, it said, "Hotel Sacher, Wien."

An envelope rested against the side and I pulled out the card. It said, "Thank you for reading my cookbook and sharing your feedback. You are truly, as your name suggests, an angel." It was signed by one of the world's most famous chefs.

"Is that what I think it is?"

I turned around. Lily, having quietly opened the door, was peeking inside.

"A Sacher-Torte," I said. "From the famous hotel in Vienna."

Lily came forward and studied the box, appreciating it. Then focused her attention on me.

"Angelica told me to come get you. People are arriving, and we're about to begin." Lily sighed. "I have a bad feeling about today, though."

"A bad feeling—why?"

"I worked so hard on my cake, but the consistency didn't come out the way I'd hoped. It's too flaky on the surface. Dry. It should be like butter all the way through" Lily bit her lip. "And it's too late to do anything now."

I turned back to the cake box on Angelica's desk. An idea came to my head, and like a drop of ink in water, it spread fast.

"What if ...?" I opened the cake box and examined the cake. A famously *perfect* cake.

We both stared at the round chocolate-covered torte, with its wax seal-like chocolate emblem on top.

"If we could remove this ..." I said.

Lily put a hand on my arm. "Bernie."

"What?"

We stared at each other for a long time. Something strange happened. It was as if I felt my own self return to my body from far, far away, and a shock, almost electric, jolted me. I was horrified at what my other half had been considering in my absence.

"Forget I ever said anything."

Lily nodded.

We left the office and headed into the cafe, where the crowd was waiting for the competition to begin.

~

The competition began.

Colorful macarons dotted a large white platter. Yellow. Lime green. Raspberry red. Pink. Brown. Cream. Angelica took a bite of the yellow one, a passion-fruit macaron, and nodded. She made a note on her legal pad. When Jerry and Mrs. Viola tasted the same one, they also seemed pleased. But no one finished the salted caramel macaron, and the Earl Grey-infused one crumbled so badly, the judges abandoned any attempts at eating it. There was a praline macaron, and that one seemed to divide the judges: Jerry liked it, Mrs. Viola was on the fence, but Angelica sighed and shook her head.

Then they turned their attention to a cake. It was a version of the classic French Opera cake, Mrs. Viola explained, if not first invented by Cyriaque Gavillon, pastry chef of Pâtisserie Dalloyau, then certainly popularized by him. The cake consisted of almond sponge layers soaked in coffee syrup, layered with ganache and French buttercream with coffee, and covered in a chocolate glaze.

Jerry took the first bite and closed his eyes, clearly savoring the taste. Little bits of it got caught in his beard. Mrs. Viola didn't close her eyes—she opened them wide with genuine surprise. Then scribbled hastily on her notepad as she muttered, "Magnificent, magnificent." Angel-ica's reaction was less dramatic. Still, she smiled, and nodded as she scribbled a few notes

Then came the chocolate torte. Now, all the entries were

anonymous, but since I'd watched Lily bake it in my kitchen, I knew this one belonged to her. Also, Lily, who stood next to me, had gone rigid and gripped my hand so hard, I was risking a fracture.

Mrs. Viola took a bite and nodded. She said, "Ah," which I took as a good sign.

Jerry forked a morsel into his mouth. Then, having tasted it, swallowed a bigger piece. Another good sign.

Finally, Angelica tasted it. She closed her eyes. She didn't even chew. It was as if she was waiting for all the flavor to spread through her mouth. Finally, she made a note on her pad, but she didn't nod or smile or do anything else.

"What does it mean?" Lily whispered.

"I don't know," I said. "They seem to like it."

"But do they love it?"

Once all the entries had been tasted, the judges huddled to talk. Their whispers at times grew loud as they disagreed, but it seemed they largely saw eye-to-eye on which baked goods had been the most successful.

Finally, Mrs. Viola, spokesperson for the judges, stood up. She opened the envelope that contained the names of the contestants and which baked goods they'd submitted.

"Though ambitious and, at times, well-executed, especially the passion fruit, Enrico Marchetti's macarons were too uneven. Some too dry. Others too bland—or, like the salt caramel, too strong. Enrico, thank you for participating."

Angelica added her thanks—and praised him for his inventiveness, adding some warmth to Mrs. Viola's cold assessment. But the implication was clear. Enrico was out. He wouldn't continue to the finals.

Enrico took his defeat with good humor. "I really messed

up the caramel. And the Earl Grey. But next time, I'll get them right."

Mrs. Viola continued her summation.

"The Opera cake was—and I don't think I'm overstating this—sublime. This is a cake that can easily turn into a second-rate layer cake. Yet Vicky Bello created a perfect balance between the flavor and texture. Even a professional patisserie chef would be proud of such an accomplishment."

Vicky beamed at the audience as she took a bow. Her mother put an arm around her and said, "We did it."

Finally, Mrs. Viola came to Lily's chocolate torte.

"This flourless chocolate torte proves that what may appear to be minimalist on the outside can contain multitudes within. The texture was nearly ruined. A cracked top showed that the crust had become too dry. Fortunately, however, the inside revealed the torte's true potential: smooth, buttery, and powerfully rich without being heavy. An excellent piece of work."

I disentangled my hand from Lily's and gave her a hug. "You did it."

As the audience applauded and congratulated the two winners, Lily let out a breath of relief. But her face still contained worry, her frown deepening as Mrs. Viola cleared her throat to get everyone's attention again.

"Whereas this round focused on the contestants' own recipes, in the finals, each of the two junior bakers will attempt a recipe nominated by the judges."

Angelica handed out two envelopes, one for Lily, the other for Vicky.

Lily tore hers open and studied the card within with fervent concentration.

"Oh," she said, then chewed her lower lip, visibly nervous.

"A difficult one?" I asked.

"I've never gotten it right ..."

Vicky looked at her card, gave it a cursory glance, and then passed it to her mom, seemingly unfazed. Then she turned to Lily with a smirk on her face.

"Can't stand the heat?"

"It's fine." Lily, staring at the recipe card, looked queasy. "It'll be fine."

Vicky snickered. "Face it, Lily. You're out of your class."

**11**

―――――

"I can't believe I was even considering it."

I shook my head and broke a pignoli cookie in two, abstaining from eating either half.

Nat's appetite wasn't affected, though. He popped a pignoli into his mouth and chewed and offered some muffled advice:

"You aren't a saint, Bernie. You're human." He finished chewing and washed the cookie down with some water. "You thought about cheating. But thinking isn't the same as doing."

Angelica came out of the back, carrying a plate with the tempting cake itself. She set it down on our table along with three plates, cake forks, and a bowl of homemade whipped cream. She sat down.

"Nat's right, Bernie. What matters is that you didn't do it. And I'm glad you didn't."

"Because it would've disappointed you."

"Because I would've known immediately what you'd done. You can't easily pass a Sacher-Torte off as your own."

She cut three slices of the cake, one for each of us, and

added a dollop of whipped cream. Then said, "Now, if you'd submitted a less well-known cake—or you'd asked me to make one for you ..."

"Would you have done that, if I asked you?

Angelica smiled. "But see, that's the thing, you never would have. Now stop worrying about it and eat your cake."

There was a knock at the door.

"Who could that be?"

Angelica got to her feet, went to the front door, and unlocked it. "We're closed for the day, but if—" Then she opened the door wide. "Gina, sweetie, please come in."

Gina Rizzoli stumbled into Moroni's. Her face was streaked with tears. She gripped one hand in the other, anxiously twisting them.

She looked at Nat and me and then around the cafe, her eyes wide and fearful, like a hunted animal.

"People know ... Mrs. Viola, she was following me ... I didn't know where to go..."

Angelica shut the door. "Come have a piece of cake."

Gently, she took Gina by the arm, led her to our table, and pulled out a chair for her. Angelica got an extra plate and cake fork and cut her a piece of pie. Then she went to the counter and got a bottle of Austrian apricot brandy, *Marillenschnaps*.

"Eat and drink first," she said. "Then talk."

Gina, in a daze, ate her cake and took a sip of the powerful liqueur. The rest of us got to taste it, too, Angelica and Nat occasionally glancing at Gina. But as I ate my own cake, I found it difficult to look over at our guest. Guilt twisted in my gut.

Halfway through her cake, Gina said, "Rob didn't kill Anne."

"We believe you," Angelica said.

"He's a pacifist. He believes God put us on Earth to spread His peace and love. When we met out west, it was through one of my few remaining friends from back home. From Carmine. And I was worried Rob would judge me. But he didn't. He knew all about the horrible thing I did, and still, he loved me. That's how he is. He sees the real you."

"He's a good man," Angelica said.

Gina nodded vigorously. "And that wire—neither of us ever saw it before. And he would never—"

Angelica touched Gina's nearest hand, which was trembling.

"We believe you," she said.

Tears trickled down Gina's face.

"This is a nightmare," she said. "Rob's still in police custody."

I felt awful. I didn't believe Roberto did it, either, and if it hadn't been for my snooping around, Chief Tedesco wouldn't have searched Roberto's suitcase and the real killer wouldn't have had an opportunity to frame him.

A suspicion niggled at the back of my mind. I shifted in my seat. Last night, I'd said I would call Chief Tedesco and tell her what I'd learned, so she could investigate Gina.

The next morning, the killer had tried to frame her. But not knowing which suitcase was hers, the killer had mixed them up, accidentally framing Roberto instead.

Only four people knew I had called Chief Tedesco. Nat and myself. And Peewee and Nino.

"Gina." I cleared my throat. "I may have, er, overheard you and Roberto talk ..."

Gina looked at me.

"Er, eavesdrop a little, you could say. Anyway, you mentioned Nino."

She studied me. Then said, "That's right—I bumped

into him in the woods. He's got a cabin out there. On the other side of the Overlook. I stumbled on it and he came out. He wasn't happy to see me. I got a real bad feeling. Like if I overstayed my welcome, he would—he would—" She shook her head. "I don't know what he would do. But something bad would happen."

"A cabin near the Overlook?" Nat looked at me. "I know exactly where that is."

~

"In several of the Frankie F. books," Nat explained as we stumbled across roots and rocks in the darkening woods, "there's a cabin, and I'm not going to tell you what happens there. Since you haven't read the books yet, I don't want to give anything away."

"It's all right. It's getting dark. We're God knows how far from civilization. I honestly don't mind a few spoilers, as long as they don't involve death and dismemberment."

"Well, then I'd better not tell you anything."

"Great."

I was beginning to wonder why we were going to visit this cabin. A more sensible plan would've been to alert Chief Tedesco to our theory that Nino had something to do with the murder, and then let her and Officers Ferrante and Fontana stagger through the dark.

But I felt guilty about what had happened the last time I shared a hunch with the police. Nino, obviously in witness protection because of some connection to organized crime, was an easy target—just as Gina had been an easy target.

Chief Tedesco had insisted Nino had put "all that" behind him. How could she be so sure, though? And there was no doubt there was something suspicious about his behavior. But Nat and I needed more than vague suspicions. We needed—

"The cabin," Nat whispered, and he pointed to a shape among the trees.

We both stopped, and I pulled Nat behind a large tree. Peeking around its side, I studied the scene in front of us.

The small, single-story log cabin sat nestled among a dense growth of trees. It had a gabled roof with crude shingles, and no visible chimney. No front porch, either. Just a log for a threshold and a narrow door. It hardly seemed suitable for living.

When I whispered my observations to Nat, he said, "Maybe it's a hunter's cabin, basically made to provide shelter, not a real home."

A window next to the front door glowed. Lights were on inside. Someone was home. As we came closer, I heard a *thwack*, followed by a long silence, and then another *thwack*.

"What is that sound?"

"Look," Nat whispered.

A shadowy figure behind the cabin swung an axe over his head and brought it down with another *thwack*.

"I only hope he's chopping wood," I said.

"Don't worry. In the books, they don't use axes to chop up bodies. They use—"

"Stop," I said. "I don't want to know."

We were fifty yards from the house, when I stepped on an old branch that broke with a loud snap. The shadowy figure lowered the axe. Then took a step backward, vanishing behind the cabin.

"Where did he go?" I whispered, my stomach turning.

"He must be back there somewhere."

We crept forward.

No sign of Nino. The door to the cabin stood ajar, light

pouring out. We skirted the cabin and came to a chopping block and a pile of firewood out back. There was a small window set in the back wall. But no Nino.

I peered through the window, seeing a bare space with scant furniture. And most importantly, no Nino.

We backtracked to the front door, moving around the cabin. With every step, my heart beat louder in my ears. Yet it seemed my feet insisted on outdoing the heavy thumping of my heart—crushing leaves and snapping twigs so loudly, it felt as if the sounds could be heard miles away.

Nat and I rounded the cabin, and I scanned the trees. In the distance, a bird trilled. A squirrel startled me as it scrambled up the trunk of a tree.

"Where did he go?" I muttered.

My stomach was turning into a sailor's knot. If the tension kept increasing, I'd need something much stronger than Austrian brandy to calm my nerves.

"Let's look inside," Nat said.

I pushed the door open, and it creaked, making the hairs on my neck stand up.

Inside was a single room. There was a military cot against the left wall. Underneath it lay a stack of towels and blankets, plus what looked like a picnic blanket bundled up. On a small folding table at the back sat a camping stove and cans of food, all neatly lined up. Against the right-hand wall stood another folding table. A notepad and pen lay on the table, lined up side by side. All along the cabin's walls stood stacks of books, neatly arranged. In spite of the spartan interior—or, in part, because of it—the place felt obsessively tidy.

"Cozy," Nat said. "Just needs a bar, Wi-Fi, and a cat, and it could be a half-decent home."

"Don't," a voice said behind us, "move."

I jumped and spun around. Nino was standing in the doorway, the axe in his hands.

I tried to smile. "Sorry, I moved."

He harrumphed and pushed past me, stomping into the cabin. Sneaking up on us, he'd not made a peep. Now he made a racket, setting down his axe against the wall, slamming a pot onto the stove and turning on the burner.

Nat nudged me. "Tattoos."

"Huh?"

Nino's shirt sleeves were rolled up, revealing tattoo-riddled arms. I didn't see the significance. But Nino apparently did, because as soon as he caught us looking, he pulled down his sleeves.

As he buttoned the shirt at his wrists, he said, "You found me. Now what do you want?"

"We thought maybe ..."

Nino glared at me. The cabin felt tiny. No, it didn't *feel* tiny. It *was* tiny. And that axe was still closer to Nino than to us. Not that I was going to dive for the axe and defend myself with it. My only defense were the pair of sneakers I wore. I only hoped they were capable of outrunning Nino—I sure didn't feel up to it.

*Stop babbling. What would Eve Silver do?*

Eve would've done a dozen things differently and caught the killer by now. At the very least, she would ask some of the many questions I had.

I straightened up, trying to look confident. Maybe I could even fool myself into believing I was confident.

"We thought we could ask you about your relationship with Anne."

"You police?"

"No."

"Didn't think so."

He turned his back on us and opened a can and poured its contents into the pot. He put down the empty can. It said, *Spaghetti & Meatballs.* Somehow seeing a grown Italian man pour canned spaghetti and meatballs into a pot made me indignant. Carlo's influence, no doubt.

In any case, it made me feel bold enough to take a step closer.

"Hey," I said. "This whole strong, silent type doesn't work on me. A woman's been murdered, and there's something you're clearly not telling us."

Nino stirred the pot. He turned around. His glare had vanished. Instead he stared at me with a cold, emotionless gaze that made my skin crawl.

I was a cockroach, and he was contemplating how to remove me.

"But," I said, taking two steps backward, and bumping into Nat, "if you value your privacy, I totally understand …"

Another thing I understood now? How Nino had rattled Gina so much. This guy was good. Either a method actor or a real-deal bad dude.

Nat came to the rescue. He snapped his fingers. "I got it now. The snake and the dragon. Those are Frankie's tattoos, aren't they?"

Nino's icy gaze faltered. He blinked.

"What?"

Nat grinned. "I knew it. I'm right. You got your arms tattooed in honor of Frankie F." He nudged me with his elbow, digging hard into my side. "Can you believe that? That's serious fandom."

"Isn't Frankie a killer?" I asked.

"Oh, yeah. Cold-blooded."

"So it's a tribute to a cold-blooded murderer?"

"One hundred percent," Nat said, still excited by his discovery.

"No," Nino cut in. "Frankie's more than that. He symbolizes light and dark. The yin and the yang."

Nat shrugged. "Well, sure. There's definitely depth to his character. But he's still a stone-hearted assassin."

"If the novels have a hero, it's Frankie."

"I'm not disputing that, Nino, but—"

"He changes." Nino wagged a finger at us. "You wait and see. He's going to change."

"Wait, you mean you know where the narrative arc is going for the whole series?" Nat slapped his forehead. "Of course you do. You must know more than anyone. Except Peewee Puglisi, of course."

"Except him, yeah."

"So," Nat said, "what did Anne know?"

"She didn't know much."

Nino frowned, seeming to realize what Nat had done—made him talk.

I saw my opening.

"Listen, Nino. I saw something the night Anne died. She put her hand in your pocket. Did she steal something from you?"

"Steal from me?" His gaze wandered from my face for an instant, as if a thought threatened to distract him. Then it came back, hard and cold. "Don't be crazy. What would she steal from me?"

I didn't have an answer to that. We stared at each other, Nino's frown growing deeper and deeper until it had returned to his dangerous glare.

"My dinner's almost ready," he said.

If he'd said, *My gun's loaded,* it couldn't have sounded more threatening.

Nat held up his hands. So did I. We backed out of the cabin.

"Great talking to you," Nat said. "Let's talk again soon. Grab a drink at the Old Mill?"

We were a few paces from the door when Nino strode toward us and my heart leaped into my throat.

He grabbed the door and with a growl, slammed it shut.

"You had me tricked, too, you know. I thought you were fanboying. Meanwhile, you were getting him to talk."

"Who was tricking anyone?" Nat said, as we made our way back to the parking lot down the Overlook trail. "I'm super excited to hear about the way Frankie's character will develop."

He winked at me.

"You never cease to amaze me," I said with a smile.

Not that we'd learned much. The most shocking revelation was that Nino Clemenza ate canned spaghetti and meatballs, which, to be fair, ought to be a crime under New Jersey's criminal code. I knew most of Carmine would back me up on that.

Why was Nino hiding out in his cabin? Maybe he wasn't hiding himself. An odd detail came back to me: the picnic blanket under the cot.

It had looked as if something were bundled up inside.

And what about his reaction to Anne putting her hand in his pocket? He'd dismissed the idea that she'd stolen from him. But something about it had distracted him. Either he didn't know what Anne had been up to—or he was lying.

My gut told me it was the latter. But why lie about someone picking your pocket?

I was contemplating this question, when my phone pinged. My screen lit up. The message was from Chief Tedesco.

> Roberto Rizzoli in the clear. Released from custody. We're back to square one …

"That's good news," Nat said.

"For Roberto and Gina, yes. But where does that leave us with the investigation?"

We emerged from the woods. At the edge of the parking lot, I noticed two cars parked near ours. Two people stood close together in the beam of light cast from inside one of the vehicles, a black SUV. It was full dark now. An unusual time to see hikers.

I was about to tell Nat this, when I recognized one of the people.

I put out an arm and blocked Nat. Then put a finger to my lips and drew him back into the shadows.

The man wore sunglasses and a baseball cap. The woman hadn't bothered hiding her identity. It was Charlene Bello—Vicky's mom. As the man handed her a thermal bag, I heard her say something, and the light catching her face revealed a mocking smile.

The man made a gesture, an Italian thing I'd seen some people in Carmine make when they were very angry. It involved swiping the fingers off the bottom of the chin. It was rude. Let's just say that Father Bruno never made that gesture.

Charlene called the man a name. Also something Father Bruno wouldn't repeat.

Then the man and Charlene got into their cars. The

man revved the engine of his black SUV and pulled out of the parking lot, followed shortly by Charlene's silver Mercedes.

"People don't usually deliver drugs in thermal bags, do they?" I said.

"Charlene Bello doesn't need to sell drugs to make money—she got a good divorce settlement. Grande is loaded."

"Grande?"

"Yeah, who else would that be?"

I continued to stare slack-jawed at Nat.

"You didn't know? Charlene's ex—Vicky's dad—is Michael Grande, the Prince of the Patisserie. Even at night, wearing sunglasses, and with a baseball cap pulled over his face, the guy's unmistakable."

"That was Michael Grande?"

Nat nodded.

I gazed off into the dark, where the cars had vanished. "Then that thermal bag definitely doesn't contain drugs."

**12**

---

Nat and I walked into the Old Mill still talking about what we'd seen in the woods—the meeting between Charlene Bello and Michael Grande, but especially our encounter with Nino Clemenza.

"What is he hiding?" I asked Nat for the umpteenth time.

"There's a guy who might be able to answer our question."

At the bar, Peewee was drinking a glass of whiskey. Or rather he was staring into the glass as he twirled the ice cubes.

"Bad day, Peewee?" Nat asked.

"Oh, hi." He smiled and pushed his big glasses up his nose. "Not a bad day, as such. Just a tough one. Slow writing days always put me in a funk."

Nat slipped onto a barstool on Peewee's right, while I took the one to the left. We both ordered red ales from Jerry. Peewee glanced at Nat, then at me.

"Why do I feel like I'm being surrounded?"

"What is Nino Clemenza hiding?"

Peewee studied me for a while.

"Honestly?" He sighed. "Who knows? The guy's an enigma wrapped inside a conundrum and dumped into a mystery."

"So you don't know."

"Oh, I didn't say that. I've got an idea that he's got a sordid past. Something to do with organized crime. And he got out of it. His name might not even be Nino Clemenza. But he's never been open to talking. And why pry?"

"Why not? You trust him with an important part of your business."

"Exactly. I don't want to scare the guy off. He's done nothing wrong." Peewee raised an eyebrow. "Has he?"

I told him about our visit to the cabin, and Nino's threatening attitude. Peewee took a sip of whiskey and stared into the middle distance.

"That's shocking," he said, "about the spaghetti and meatballs."

He guffawed, showing his big teeth.

"But seriously, from where I'm sitting you're simply describing my research assistant. Mr. Antisocial has always been like that."

"All right," I said. "Then what about Anne picking Nino's pocket, and Nino claiming to know nothing about it? Plus, there's this picnic blanket at the cabin and something's bundled inside ..."

Peewee furrowed his brows. "What do you mean, she picked his pocket?"

I described what I'd seen at Milano Books, the drunken Anne sticking her hand into Nino's pocket as he carried her into the back office.

"So, what did she steal from Nino?"

"It makes no sense," Peewee said. "But look, Nino and I

have a meeting tomorrow morning. I'll talk to him about this whole pickpocketing business. He can be stubborn—but he and I have a good relationship. I'll get him to talk." He downed his whiskey and got up to go. "Promise."

⁓

After Peewee left, Nat finished his drink.
"Head home?"
I shook my head. "You go. I'll stay for a while." We said our goodbyes.

I wanted time to think. I was relieved that Roberto Rizzoli had been released. The whole discovery of the murder weapon had been far too convenient. Increasingly, my instinct told me to look at Nino Clemenza—as Gina had said, something about him was *off*.

Jerry asked me if I wanted another drink. I ordered a seltzer. I didn't need alcohol to cloud my thoughts right now.

As I was sipping my bubbly water, Primo Leone came into the Old Mill and sat down a couple of stools over from me.

He and Jerry talked. Or rather, Primo talked and Jerry nodded silently.

Watching Primo, I was reminded of Father Bruno's story of the mafioso who'd left his crime family to take a new path in life. Well, Primo had done that. For a moment, I wondered if Father Bruno's story had actually been about him. Maybe. In any case, Primo had faced a similar change in his life, leaving one life for another.

Primo always seemed content, even happy. It was as if driving a taxi in a small town in New Jersey was the perfect occupation for him. But driving had also been his job in the

mafia. He'd changed paths, yes, but the two paths had similarities.

Jerry wandered off to restock some of the shelves, and I
took the opportunity to talk to Primo.

"Primo, do you mind if I ask you something personal?"

"Sure thing, Bernie."

"When you changed careers ..."

I felt my face grow warm. I didn't know how to ask this
in a delicate way. Fortunately, Primo came to the rescue.

"You mean when I stopped driving a car for *la famiglia*,
and instead became a cab driver in Carmine?"

I nodded. "I'm wondering how you made the decision. I
mean, was it hard? Was it even dangerous?"

"Ah, you watch too much TV, Bernie. Not everyone who
works for the mafia and then leaves ends up in a ditch. I was
a chauffeur. Then I said, 'Fellas, I gotta be doing something
else.' They said, 'Sure, Primo. You go ahead.'"

"But what about personally? Was it difficult to figure out
who the new you was—the new Primo?"

"Primo's Primo," he said with a grin. "But I get what
you're asking. And I guess it took time for me to settle down.
You know, I still see some of the old *paesans*. What they tell
me—" He shook his head. "—it don't make me miss the old
life."

"Like what you told me about Mad Mouse Manzo."

"Yeah, like that."

We finished our drinks, and then Primo offered to drive
me home again. I insisted on paying. He ran a taxi service,
after all.

"Fuhgeddaboudit, Bernie. When I'm off duty, I'm off
duty."

We said goodnight to Jerry and went outside. The air
was chilly. The nights were getting cooler and cooler. In a

few weeks, we'd all be wearing coats. Then the first signs of winter would come.

The gravel in the parking lot crunched beneath our feet.

Primo insisted I get in the passenger seat, since tonight wasn't a taxi ride.

We rode down the hill toward Carmine in companionable silence. But all the while I was thinking about Mad Mouse Manzo and the kinds of stories Primo heard from his old *paesans* in the mafia world.

"Primo, do you think this murder's got anything to do with the mafia?"

"Did the bosses put a hit out on this Anne Adams? Or even put a hit out on Peewee Puglisi because of his books, and then some *mamaluke* messed it up and whacked the wrong person?" He shook his head. "I don't believe it. If the bosses wanted to kill Peewee, they woulda done it by now. And why kill his book agent? She ain't connected." He stared out at the road, pursing his lips. Then said, "Except ..."

We'd passed Moroni's and now he turned off Garibaldi Avenue and onto Da Vinci Street.

"Except what?"

"Well, Mad Mouse Manzo had this crazy thing for the wire, you know, and strangling. Which is why when the murder happened, the idea that Manzo was involved maybe wasn't so crazy."

"But he's dead."

"Very dead. Still, there's another guy ..."

"Another mafia guy who likes to use the garrote wire?"

"He used to like wires and guns and knives, all kinds of weapons. The bosses loved him, because he was so tidy, you know. Clean. Left everything shipshape."

Primo shook his head.

"But again, he wouldn't have killed Anne Adams, and screwing up trying to kill Peewee, that's not like him. Plus, the guy got locked up years ago."

"So there's no chance he'd be out again?"

"Well, I hear he cut a deal with the Feds ..."

We turned onto Lampedusa Lane, and Primo pulled the car into my driveway.

"Home sweet home," he said.

"Thanks for the ride."

I unbuckled my seat belt and got out of the car and said goodnight, but before closing the door, I ducked down to ask Primo another question.

"This mafia guy—what's his name?"

"DeGrazio," Primo said. "Giannino DeGrazio."

As I walked to my door, I kept thinking about the name. DeGrazio. Wasn't that the guy Father Bruno had told me about—the one who'd changed paths?

## 13

The two cakes sat in the middle of the judges' table. One was a torte with a complex latticework of pastry, covering a layer of red jam and dusted with powdered sugar.

"Linzer torte," Mrs. Viola explained in a schoolmarmish voice. "One of the oldest cakes in the world. Also one of the more difficult ones to make, since the crumbly pastry crust must be just so, especially since the baker must fold the strips of pastry into a web. The crust consists of ground almonds or hazelnuts, flavored with cinnamon, lemon zest, and cloves. The risk is that this delicate concoction falls apart in the oven—or once it's removed."

Angelica, Mrs. Viola, and Jerry each took a bite of the Linzer torte, none of them aware of who had created it— Lily or Vicky. I studied the finalists' faces. Lily looked nervous. Vicky looked smug.

As the judges made notes on legal pads and whispered to each other, there was a lot of head nodding and fork wagging.

Then they turned their attention to the second cake,

and Mrs. Viola cleared her throat to deliver another lesson. This cake was even more impressive looking. It seemed to be covered in chocolate and topped with a thick caramel glaze.

"The famous Dobos torte from Hungary. Delicate layers of sponge cake filled with chocolate buttercream and topped with a caramel-glazed layer that is cut into triangular wedges. If the baker fails to maintain precise control over temperature and timing, the whole thing cracks or, even worse, burns."

Each judge in turn sliced off a small piece with their forks and took a bite. Angelica pursed her lips. Mrs. Viola closed her eyes. Jerry nodded his head, as if in rhythm to music no one else could hear.

In fact, no music played at Moroni's that morning. A crowd had gathered, much bigger for the finals than the semi-finals, and people stood shoulder-to-shoulder, wall-to-counter. Yet no one spoke. It seemed everyone held their breath. Well, I can't speak for everyone. I know I held my breath. I hardly dared move a limb, afraid to disrupt the almost sacred atmosphere.

Then there was more scribbling on the notepads, and the judges conferred.

Mrs. Viola got to her feet.

"The judges are in agreement, and the winning torte is —" She paused. Maybe for a few seconds. It felt like minutes. Hours. My lungs screamed for air. My right foot began to tap the floor of its own volition, and I was about to curse it, when Mrs. Viola finished her sentence. "—the Dobos torte."

"Yes!"

Vicky Bello shot to her feet and punched the air.

"Yes, yes, yes!"

She grinned at her mom, and Charlene threw her arms around her daughter and they danced together.

"We won, we won," they both chanted.

Frowns from several people. Not everyone appreciated such self-congratulatory winners. But Angelica played her part beautifully. She smiled.

"Of course, we must add that the Linzer torte was a close second. This cake showed exceptional talent—the kind of remarkable execution that is rare in someone so young."

Both Mrs. Viola and Jerry nodded, agreeing with Angelica's statement.

Lily got up from her chair and held out her hand to Vicky.

"Well done, Vicky," she said. "Congratulations—your torte is incredible. You deserve to win."

Vicky snorted, ignoring Lily's hand.

"Where's my diploma?"

I brought out the oversized diplomas that I'd prepared for the two finalists, first handing one to Lily, which said, "Lily Salerno: Second Place at Carmine's Junior Baking Competition." She thanked me and then thanked the three judges.

I handed the other diploma to Vicky.

It said, "Victoria Grande: First Place at Carmine's Junior Baking Competition."

When she saw it, Vicky frowned. "This is wrong. You got my name wrong."

Charlene stepped closer and yanked the diploma from her daughter's hands. "Vicky changed her name after my husband and I divorced. I can't believe you messed this up. How disrespectful. What kind of amateur show are you running here? I want this changed at once. At once!"

"I can explain," I said calmly. "I put Victoria Grande

instead of Bello. It only seemed fitting that Vicky use her father's name since the cake itself says—" I stepped over to the judges' table, grabbed the cake, which elicited a gasp from the audience, and flipped it over on its head. "— Michael Grande."

And there it was, as I'd known it would be. The bottom was signed with a thin chocolate script—a distinctive curlicue that said,

*Michael Grande*

Grande always insisted on signing his cakes. Even when he was helping his daughter cheat.

"Under different circumstances, this could've been a beautiful story about two adults reconciling as they supported their daughter to pursue her passion for baking." I shook my head. "But sadly, Charlene Bello and Michael Grande's only interest in working together was this: They wanted their little Vicky to win at all costs."

Vicky yelled at her mom, "I told you! I told you and Daddy this was a dumb idea—look what's happened now ..."

"Shut up, Vicky," Charlene hissed. "They can't prove a thing."

Angelica firmly grasped the diploma and pulled it from Charlene's hands. "I think we just did," she said. Then shocked everyone by tearing it in two.

It was as if someone had fired a starter pistol. Pandemonium broke out: Charlene protesting her innocence, Vicky yelling at her mom, Mrs. Viola lecturing on the sins of cheating, her finger raised at the Bellos, while people in the crowd talked—some even hurling Italian insults at the Bellos.

While the din in the cafe grew louder and louder, the arm waving more and more dramatic, I enjoyed the madness. But above all, I enjoyed watching Angelica pull Lily aside, and hand her the first-prize diploma. I'd already prepared it that morning, carefully writing out her name.

Lily's eyes teared up. Because of the noise, I couldn't hear what she was muttering, but I could guess: *I can't believe it, I can't believe it.*

Jerry put an arm around her and said, "Believe it, kid. You won fair and square, and deserve a hundred diplomas for that cake of yours."

My jaw dropped. Jerry never said so many words at one time. Maybe he felt safe breaking character because almost no one could hear him. I could, though. And he knew that. He winked at me, and pushed his way through the crowd toward the exit, no doubt heading back to the Old Mill.

"He's right, you know," Angelica said to Lily. "Your cake was amazing and nearly beat the great Michael Grande."

I was about to add my own congratulations, when my phone vibrated in my pocket. I dug it out and put a hand to my other ear, trying to hear what the person at the other end was saying.

"What was that?" I yelled into the phone.

I had to step behind the counter and into the corridor in the back to hear.

"Can you say that again?"

"Bernie," Nat yelled back. "Drop everything."

"Nat, where were you? I thought you'd be at the competition."

"Come to the public library *now*."

"What? Why?"

"I found our killer."

Like a card dealer, Nat dealt out photographs and printouts of newspaper articles on the table in the tiny historical society exhibition space. More and more papers covered the surface.

"What is all this?" I asked.

"Last night, after leaving you at the Old Mill, I went home. But I couldn't sleep. So I came back here."

"You went to work?"

"And I stayed all night."

His appearance confirmed it. His hair, usually so floppy, stuck out to the sides. His glasses were smudged. His flannel shirt crumpled.

"Nat, you need a change of clothes, a hot shower, and some coffee."

"Later," he said, and gestured at the papers on the table. "After our encounter with Nino in the woods, I couldn't stop thinking about something."

"The canned spaghetti and meatballs."

"His tattoos. He's got a snake on one arm and a dragon on the other. That's similar to the description of Frankie F.'s tattoos."

He reached across the table. A tall stack of books leaned precariously on the edge. He grabbed the top one, which had several sticky notes stuck inside as bookmarks. He flipped the book open.

"Here on page 79: He stared down at his bloody hands. The splatter had dappled his tattoos: a snake curling around a sword on one arm, a dragon curling around a tree on the other."

"That does sound like Nino's tattoos. But that's hardly

strange. The guy doesn't just spend his life researching plots for Peewee, he seems obsessed with Frankie F."

"That's what I thought. A tribute to Frankie, the character, right? Only Mrs. Viola had me going over murder cases of the past 20 years. I'm pretty sure she did it so I could dig up stuff on Rita Glen, since she was convinced Gina murdered Anne and framed Roberto. But I found something else, too."

He handed me a printout. It was a photograph that had been blown up and the picture was grainy as a result.

"A pair of arms? With tattoos? Oh." I squinted, studying the tattoos. "Now I see. Snake and dragon. It's a photo of Nino Clemenza."

"This is from ten years ago. Before the first Frankie F. novel."

"Before it was written?"

"Yes, *before*."

Nat snatched the paper out of my hands. Then handed me another.

This time the photograph was much larger. The man in the photograph was wearing a tank top and black slacks. He wore sunglasses.

"It's Nino. Wait—"

I looked closer.

"It's not."

"What made you change your mind? The nose, right?"

"Yeah, the nose is different."

Nat, excited, riffled through the papers on the table and brought up another.

"Now look at this one."

Same guy. Same nose. But no sunglasses this time.

"Those eyes," I said, and shuddered. "If it weren't for the nose, he'd be Nino's double. Who is he?"

Nat handed me another sheet of paper. This time a printout of a newspaper article. It said, "Notorious mob hitman testifies for prosecution." The photo showed the same guy—Nino's double—in a suit and tie.

"He cut a deal," Nat said. "And then disappeared."

"Right into witness protection."

"You bet. But not before visiting a plastic surgeon for a nose job."

I let out a low whistle. "Nino Clemenza really does have a big secret."

"Except that's not his name."

I looked down the article and found the hitman's name. Then stared up at Nat.

"Giannino DeGrazio?"

"Also known as 'Nino.' Remember what Frankie F.'s full name is?"

"Frankie Fazio." The pieces of the puzzle fit nearly together. I smacked my forehead, seeing the truth. "Frankie Fazio and Nino DeGrazio. They're one and the same."

I stared at the newspaper clipping, incredulous at what we'd discovered. But then it made so much sense. Peewee knew all along what Nino's true identity was. Maybe he hired Nino as a research assistant, stumbled on the truth, and then had a great idea: Why not turn fact into fiction?

"I wonder if he keeps that cabin in the woods as a place to hide out in case his enemies discover where he's hiding. I bet a lot of mobsters would love to know where Nino DeGrazio is."

"Who's Nino DeGrazio?"

I jumped.

Mrs. Viola stood behind me, craning her neck to see the papers scattered on the table. She frowned.

"I'm sorry about the mess, Mrs. Viola," Nat said. "I'll clean it up as soon as I can."

But Mrs. Viola ignored him. "The police have released Roberto. Chief Tedesco insists Gina didn't do it, and all right, I admit I was wrong. But someone framed my Rob, and I won't stand for it. I'll give that killer a smacking they'll never forget. Now, tell me what you know."

Nat explained what he'd discovered about Nino Clemenza actually being Nino DeGrazio, the former mafia hitman. "And if Anne Adams found out …"

"Then Nino had a strong motive to silence her," Mrs. Viola said.

"Peewee lied," I added. "He knew about Nino. But he doesn't know Nino killed Anne. They're meeting this morning, and he's going to push Nino to tell the truth. How do you think Nino will react?"

Nat frowned. "Nino's going to shut him up."

~

The old Honda Accord swung wildly as Nat spun the steering wheel and we careened onto the street where Nino lived. The tie-dye dice hanging from the rearview mirror swung back and forth. The car shot forward, and Nat turned the wheel, preparing to swerve into the driveway, when a massive white vehicle, appearing from out of nowhere, came barreling toward us.

I screamed. Nat did too.

Then the USPS truck screeched as it cut us off and came to a standstill in the driveway.

Roberta jumped out.

I got out of Nat's Honda Accord, my heart still pounding.

"Mrs. Viola called me," Roberta said as Nat and I joined her. "She suggested Nino was *in some* kind of *trouble*."

"Making trouble is more like it," I said. Then added, "Hey, how do you know Mrs. Viola?"

Roberta, ignoring me, strode to the front door and dug out a key and opened it. I followed, thinking—not for the first time—that Roberta's connection to Carmine went deeper than she would admit.

Inside, the house was still.

"Nino?" she called out.

Roberta headed for the kitchen. I moved into the living room, Nat close behind.

Everything was as immaculately tidy as before.

"I'll check the bedroom," Nat said.

"Be careful."

Too often in *Silver & Gold*, this was the scene where Adam Gold and Eve Silver stumbled on something horrifying, like another dead body. Or where they walked into a trap.

While Roberta and Nat searched the house, I caught sight of Nino's computer.

The screen saver bounced back and forth, as I sat down in Nino's chair. I touched the mouse and the password screen came alive.

I tried the old classic password: 1, 2, 3, 4.

It didn't work. No surprise there. Nino was meticulous. He probably had a crazy difficult password—all symbols and nonsensical code—the kind to make a cyber security expert proud.

In any case, I tried "Frankie."

That didn't work, either.

Roberta came into the living room.

"Stop playing around, Bernie," she said. "The password is *Mightier_thn_Sword*9*."

I typed in the password and got in. "Is there anything about our private lives you don't know, Roberta?"

"You're no longer in witness protection," she said. "So in theory, I know nothing."

*In theory.* That was reassuring.

I looked through Nino's files. Lots of folders with research. Lots of folders with draft manuscripts, from version one through 20-something.

But nothing suspicious.

"We've got to go find Nino," Roberta said.

"Just one more minute. If we can find evidence ..."

"His kitchen," Nat said, shaking his head as he joined us, "it's full of cans of spaghetti with meatballs. That seems to be the only thing the guy eats." He leaned over my shoulder. "Oh, try his email."

I opened the email application. Nino's emails were mostly related to research, requesting information from public authorities, contacting journalists to check facts. The rest were between him and Peewee.

"Nothing," Roberta said. "Now let's go."

"Wait."

I double clicked on the trash can, opening Nino's deleted items.

I ran a search.

And there it was. Three days before the event at Milano Books, Nino had sent an email with a manuscript attached to Peewee with Anne on copy. The reply to Nino from Anne didn't include Peewee.

I know what's going on and who you are—we need to meet. And talk business. Call me.

"That's it," I said. "Anne must've somehow discovered Nino's true identity and decided to blackmail him. So he killed her."

"Well, it's no smoking gun," Roberta said.

"Or smoking garrote wire," Nat said.

"Look at the flip calendar on the desk. Nino did call Anne, and they arranged to meet the next week. But he crossed it out."

"Because she was dead?" Nat asked.

"No. Because Nino realized Milano Books would be the perfect place to kill her—lots of suspects." I closed down the application. "Look, we need to find Nino and Peewee before it's too late."

**14**

———

We agreed that Nino and Peewee would be in one of two places: Peewee's home on Cedar Hill or Nino's cabin in the woods. After calling the police, Roberta suggested we split up, or we might not get to the right place in time to stop another murder from happening.

I suggested flipping a coin. But Roberta, jumping into the USPS truck, said, "I'll go to Puglisi's home. You check out the cabin."

In the car, Nat turned on the ignition, and pushed his hair out of his eyes. "You might've lost a coin toss, anyway."

"I would've found a way to fudge it."

"Eve Silver never fudges."

He was right, of course. I would no sooner fudge a coin flip with my friends than I would help Lily cheat at a baking competition.

"I just don't like that cabin. It's creepy."

"One man's creepy is another man's cozy."

"You forgot about one woman—this woman."

We drove out of town, taking the twisty and hillocky Lake Road, past Lake Carmine, and deeper into the woods. The gravel crunched underneath the car's tires as we pulled into the parking lot for the Overlook trail.

No Charlene Bello and Michael Grande today. But next to an old Buick I didn't recognize, there was a big, black SUV. Peewee's.

Nat and I looked at each other. "They're here."

"But whose Buick is that?" I asked.

"No idea. Mrs. Viola owns a Buick, but I haven't seen Nino in a car. He's always hitching a ride with Peewee."

I called Roberta, got her voicemail, left a message telling her what we'd discovered. Then got out of the car.

Nat said, "We're going out to the cabin, aren't we?"

I nodded. "We can't wait for Roberta or Chief Tedesco to get here. What if something happens to Peewee? We've got to move on this, and fast."

We trekked into the woods, taking the trail that led to the Overlook. Halfway up, there was a turnoff. A small, unofficial track. After a quarter of a mile on this track, we trudged off into the forest, following nothing but our deep, instinctual sense of direction ...

Well, that and my phone. I'd dropped a pin on my map app, showing me where we'd found Nino's cabin last time.

I stared at my screen and pointed ahead.

"It should be up there."

"I think I recognize the trees," Nat said.

"I definitely recognize the trees. And they're identical to the other five thousand we've already passed. Now, come on. The phone says it isn't far."

We came to the clearing with the cabin. In daytime, it was a little less creepy. *In theory*, as Roberta would say.

Because the door was shut, and I worried what we might find inside, and that made me no less worried than the last time we visited this place.

As we crept closer, I heard raised voices. Nat and I exchanged a glance.

It was at times like these that I remembered Eve Silver's gun. Whenever the music got ominous on the show, she'd pull out her gun and sneak to the nearest corner, so she could peek around and spot the bad guys.

But I didn't have a gun. And I didn't even have a corner.

Nat and I hesitated outside the door.

There was a crash inside the cabin. Something thudded against the door. Then another crash. Muffled voices. Then a loud curse word in Italian.

Nat nodded at me as I grabbed the door handle.

I pushed the door open.

Inside, Peewee and Nino were on the floor, wrestling, rolling back and forth. They both had their hands on a gun.

I looked around for a weapon.

And gasped.

On the small desk lay the picnic blanket I'd seen under Nino's cot—now unbundled to reveal the object that he'd hidden within: Anne's briefcase, and its hinged lid stood wide open.

The men rolled over, Nino getting the upper hand.

"He's going to kill me!" Peewee cried. "Help!"

"Shut up!" Nino roared.

I jumped over the two men and got to the table with the camping stove. Light from the cabin's rear window poured down on my only weapon. I gripped a rock-hard can of spaghetti and meatballs in my hand. Tested its weight. Bit my lip. Tried not to think of how hard this might hurt a human being, and then raised my arm.

I slammed it down on Nino's head.

*Thwack.*

He groaned and fell sideways.

For a moment, Nino lay halfway across Peewee, and the famous author didn't move. Then he pushed the ex-hitman off, Nino's big body landing with a soft thud.

Scrambling to his feet, Peewee turned to the briefcase. And toward me. Because I was already standing next to it, looking inside at its contents. Whatever was in this briefcase, it must be why Anne had been murdered.

To my surprise, it wasn't anything shocking.

It was just the printout of a manuscript with editorial comments. The front page bore a title and the name of the author, Marco Puglisi. And it said, in the top right-hand corner, "version #1." But as I flipped through the pages and looked at the comments between Peewee and Nino, the evidence emerged, word for word, of why Anne had been murdered.

I looked up at Peewee.

"These comments," I said. "They're all from Nino, explaining his choices. Why he wrote what he wrote. Prepping you. There's even a mention of what you can tell journalists about the upcoming book. You didn't write this novel, Peewee. In fact, you didn't write any of the novels, did you?"

With one hand, Peewee pushed his glasses up his nose. With the other, he pointed the gun at me.

"Bravo," he said. "And now you die."

~

Peewee gestured with the gun and Nat followed his instructions, tying a final knot on the ropes around Nino, binding him to a chair. He was still unconscious. That can of spaghetti and meatballs was more dangerous than I'd thought.

"Now tie your friend up," Peewee told Nat.

"Who's going tie me up?" Nat asked. "I don't want to be the odd man out."

"After I shoot you, I'll tie you up."

"That's nice of you."

There was only one chair in the cabin, and Nino was already sitting in that one, so Nat began tying me up to one of the legs of the desk. It wouldn't hold me for long. But Peewee had explained that he was going to shoot us and then burn down the cabin. So I guess the knots didn't need to be worthy of the Navy.

"Anne found out about your arrangement," I said.

"Nino, that idiot," Peewee said, grimacing. "He copied her on an email by accident. She reached out to him. Demanded to meet. But see, Nino had no interest in the truth coming out. He had a comfortable life. He couldn't write his books openly, anyway. And if he tried, I would make a few phone calls and have his old friends from the mafia make a house call."

"I thought she was blackmailing Nino. But you were the one blackmailing Nino. And she was actually trying to help him."

"Help him," Peewee said, "or destroy me. Anne was only helpful when she knew it hurt someone else. Either way, I couldn't let her go through with it."

"When did you find out? At Milano Books?"

He shook his head. "The day before. Nino confessed to

me, reassuring me that he'd talked to Anne and he'd talk to her again at their meeting the next week. But I convinced him to cancel that. I made him think I had dealt with the issue."

"He never suspected you?"

"Sure he did," Peewee said. "But what could he do? If he turned me in, I would tattle to his friends in the mafia. Nino's always been a good boy. Always protecting our mutual secrets. You know, after I failed to open Anne's briefcase, he was the one who stole it, knowing there was incriminating evidence within. And in so doing, he did me a favor. If that briefcase had been found by the police, my whole house of cards would've collapsed."

"Of course," I said. "Anne didn't pick Nino's pocket. She put something into the pocket. The key to her briefcase."

"Right. And once you told me that you saw her do that, I knew at once that Nino had the briefcase. Our secret was safe. But when I came to see him, he was talking about taking it to the police. He was using it to tip the scales—and take control of his situation." He tsk-tsked. "Nino's whole fad with going straight and narrow has gone to his head. After talking to that Father Bruno, he's thinking more and more like an upstanding citizen, not like the mobster he really is. From the beginning, I knew he was a risk. So I kept him close. And I kept you even closer."

I winced as Nat pulled the rope tight around me, and he whispered, "Keep talking."

"You couldn't get close to Chief Tedesco," I continued, "so you went for second best. Me. You knew Tedesco and I are friends, and that I would report back to her. She didn't see you as a prime suspect. And with my help, you managed to keep the focus on others."

Peewee's eyes twinkled behind his glasses—he seemed

more proud of the crime he'd committed and how he'd covered it up than the books he'd pretended to write.

I continued: "First Mad Mouse Manzo. What did you do, send the fake death threat to your fan mail address, which Nino checks? I thought so. Then, when that didn't work, you pointed me in the direction of Gina—aka Rita Glen. Anne did say, *He'll cheat again*. But you saw an opportunity."

Peewee grinned. "Thanks to my creative mind."

"And then accidentally framed Roberto."

Peewee's expression soured. "That was bad luck. If I'd put the evidence in the right suitcase, no one would've doubted Gina did it."

"You overestimate your plotting abilities," I said, and winced as Nat finished tying the rope around me. "Tedesco's no fool."

"Sadly, that's true. But I did send her off on a wild goose chase, suggesting that thriller writer in Livingston was guilty. He was lucky enough to be invited to the book event, supposedly by Anne, his ex-agent."

"But she didn't, did she? You invited him. You set him up."

"After Nino brought Anne to Phil's office, I told the guy the back office was the restroom, so he chose the wrong door, raising suspicion. A little later, I went to the restroom, making sure people saw me go in. Then, while everyone's attention was elsewhere, I snuck out and slipped into the office. Killed Anne. Tried to open her briefcase with one of her hairpins. But then someone came looking for me, and I had to get out of there." He sighed. "I tried everything I could to divert the police from suspecting me. I even began to plant small clues pointing to Nino."

"The book on garotting in his home," I said. "You left that out."

"I did. It's not like Nino to leave stuff lying around. I knew you'd get suspicious, though, and you did. Especially when he got annoyed at the book lying around."

"He wasn't worried the book was incriminating. It irritated him it was untidy."

"I'll tell you what's irritating: a barista who sticks her nose in other people's business. I'll enjoy setting fire to you and this entire mess."

I tried not to glance at Nat. He'd inched his way toward the door.

"But Peewee, why would you get rid of Nino?" I said, trying to buy us time. "You're killing the goose that lays the golden eggs."

"Sure, Nino has been a big help. But I can write books, too. And now I've got a big name—people will read anything I write."

I briefly reflected on the dangers of writerly hubris and wondered how long it would take Peewee to destroy the reputation for great books that Nino had created. Probably not long.

"Stop right there," Peewee said, swinging the gun over to point at Nat. "Don't think I don't see you. There's no escaping. And no one will come to your rescue. No, we're all alone out here in the woods. We're—"

"Nino Clemenza," a voice called outside. "This is the police. We have the cabin surrounded."

A smile spread across Peewee's face.

"Perfect timing."

He moved over to the camping stove and from behind the stack of cans, he brought out a bottle of lighter fluid and a box of matches. He stood in the light of the window, fumbling with the matches, and he called out, "Nino's going to kill us! He's setting fire to the cabin!"

He chuckled as he lit a match.

"Bye, bye, Bernie."

As held out the match and the bottle of lighter fluid, a triumphant, donkey-ish grin formed on his face.

Then glass exploded across the room.

Something flew through the back window and Peewee staggered backward.

A piece of firewood rolled across the floor. Another went flying through the broken window, and this one struck Peewee, too, and he cried out, "It hurts! It hurts!"

Outside, raised voices and confused yelling. Footfall on crackling leaves. Someone barking orders.

Nat was by my side in an instant, undoing the knots he'd tied.

Then the cabin door was ripped open, and Mrs. Viola stood in the doorway wielding a log. She was the one who'd thrown firewood through the window.

"Peewee Puglisi," she growled. "How dare you ...?"

Peewee curled up against the cot. He hugged his knees to his body and blubbered, "No, no, please ..."

He'd forgotten all about the gun. As soon as I was free, I made a move to grab it. But Nino suddenly shook off his bonds, rolled over, and grabbed the pistol.

He got into a crouch and pointed the gun at Peewee.

"Don't," he hissed, "move."

It was quite a picture. Mrs. Viola brandishing a log, Nino covering Peewee with a gun, and then Roberta LaRosa and Chief Tedesco barging through the doorway. Their faces showed surprise. Then both of them regained control and told Nino and Mrs. Viola to put down their weapons. Officers Fontana and Ferrante joined the crowd in the tiny cabin.

"I didn't do anything," Peewee said. "Nino's the killer ..."

Chief Tedesco slapped a pair of handcuffs on his wrists.

"No, you can't do this. I'm famous!"

"You have the right to remain silent ..."

And how appropriate—because now that Nino would no longer write his books for him, Peewee would, in fact, remain silent.

## 15

At Moroni's, I sliced off a piece of Lily's Linzer torte and forked it into my mouth. The buttery, nutty pastry crust fell apart in my mouth, leaving a hint of spice from cinnamon, lemon zest, and cloves. The red currant jam provided a sour, fruity contrast.

At any time, this torte would've been incredible. But today it tasted even better. Cake tastes even more amazing when you've had a brush with death.

My companions seemed to feel the same, because we ate our cake in silence.

On either side of me sat Nat and Angelica. Chief Tedesco sat next to Roberta. And then there was Nino Clemenza.

I sipped my coffee and asked the question that had been on my mind for the past hour: "So, what happens now?"

"Well, for one, Mrs. Viola ought to receive a medal," Nat said. "She figured out Peewee was the killer before the rest of us did."

Nat was right. The eccentric Mrs. Viola—once she'd been able to see past her jealousy toward Gina—had put the puzzle together. She'd told us that the connection between Nino DeGrazio and Frankie Fazio had made her consider who stood to lose the most if the truth came out: Peewee Puglisi. Once she came to that realization, she began to wonder whether Peewee, whose early books had been garbage (her words, not mine), could really have written all those bestsellers.

"She's really turned out to be a talented sleuth," I said. "But what happens to the famous Marco Puglisi?"

"Peewee goes to prison," Chief Tedesco said. "And good riddance."

Roberta said, "His publisher has their lawyers trying to figure out what to do with the royalties, since Puglisi never wrote the books. And then there's the advance on the rights for the TV adaptation. Really, the royalties should go to Nino."

"I don't want them," Nino said. "Tell them, Roberta."

Roberta nodded. Apparently she'd become Nino's spokesperson. "If the publisher will pay Nino, he'll be putting the proceeds into a charitable trust to support the victims of organized crime, and their families. Any future royalties for other books he writes will go into the trust, too."

I nodded. Nino's ascetic lifestyle meant he didn't need much, but I suspected he also felt he had a lot of penance to pay for his years of crime.

"So can we expect a new installment in the Frankie F. saga?" Nat asked.

Nino shook his head. "I'm done with Frankie. And done with Puglisi."

"He's been working on a new series," Roberta said. "It's historical, set in Victorian England, and features a country doctor who investigates crimes. No blood and gore."

"A historical cozy mystery?" Nat sounded incredulous.

"Ooh, that sounds good," I said.

"Look for it in your local bookstore," Roberta said. "But not under the name Nino Clemenza, of course."

She wouldn't divulge the name. But I could imagine it would be nothing like his current name. First his nose, now his subject matter. What would be left once Nino stripped himself of his past? I had a feeling one thing would remain.

"Nino, I've got to know. What's the deal with the canned spaghetti and meatballs?"

"I developed a taste for it in prison. I kinda prefer it now."

I shook my head. There was no accounting for taste.

Nino took his last bite of torte and licked his lips, and looked at Roberta. "Time to go?"

Roberta nodded.

Nino got to his feet and shook everyone's hand, one by one.

"Where are you going?" I asked.

"He can't tell you that," Roberta said. "But it should appeal to his love of nature. A rustic cabin. Lots of wood to chop. And snow shoes."

I shuddered. I knew exactly where Nino was going. Roberta had nearly sent me to that cabin in the farthest flung north of Alaska. But if Nino was worried about frost bite, he didn't show it. He smiled. And I realized that an isolated cabin in Alaska with lots of books and no one to talk to was Nino's idea of heaven.

Roberta and Nino walked out of Moroni's, leaving the rest of us to finish Lily's cake.

Moroni's. My friends. And a delicious cake.

That was my idea of heaven.

"Angelica," I said. "I want to apologize."

"What in the world do you want to apologize for?"

"I've been so absent from work." I looked down at my cake plate. "As usual."

Angelica reached over and took my hand.

"Can I tell you a secret? I told you to go with Peewee when he asked you to join him for his amateur investigation. I encouraged you to leave early after you went to Lakeview. I never called you back to Moroni's when you ran off to meet Nat after the competition. Why?"

I shrugged. "I don't know."

"Because I knew you needed to go. I knew it was important."

"But so is Moroni's."

"And Moroni's will be here whenever you come back. *Mia cara,* what matters the most to me is that you are happy. If a fairy godmother granted me one wish, do you know what it would be?"

"An endless supply of cannoli?" Nat quipped.

"She's already got that covered," I said.

"I would wish," Angelica said, ignoring us, "for everyone I love to be happy."

She hugged me, and I hugged her. Angelica would never be visited by a fairy godmother because, frankly, she was the fairy godmother. I squeezed her tight. Then I felt Nat's arms around us.

"Hey," he said, squeezing us both, "no way I'm losing out on this love fest."

I closed my eyes, savoring the hug. I was right where I belonged.

Thank you for reading. Please subscribe to my newsletter to get a FREE short story, plus updates on new books and special deals: https://mpblackbooks.com/newsletter/

## THE END

# ABOUT THE AUTHOR

M.P. Black writes fun cozies with an emphasis on food, books, and travel — and, of course, a good old murder mystery.

In addition to writing and publishing his own books, he helps others fulfill their author dreams too.

M.P. Black has lived in many places, including Austria, Costa Rica, and the United Kingdom. Today, he lives in Copenhagen, Denmark, with his family.

Join M.P. Black's free newsletter for updates on books and special deals:

https://mpblackbooks.com/newsletter/